An Elemental Fire

Carol R. Ward

Lois,

May the flames of fortune burn brighter for you.

An Elemental Fire
ISBN :1937477606
An Elemental Fire Copyright © 2012 Carol R. Ward
Published by Brazen Snake Books

Cover art by Heidi Sutherlin

This book is a work of fiction and any resemblance to persons, living or dead, or places, events or locales is purely coincidental. The characters are productions of the author's imagination, and used fictitiously.

Dedication

To all of you who read An Elemental Wind and
immediately asked,
"When's the next one coming out?"

Acknowledgments

Thank you to Jamie DeBree, who continues to be
a pillar of strength in support of my insanity. Thank
you to Heidi Sutherlin, for her awesome work on my
cover.

And a special shout-out to my betas: Jamie,
Karin, and Steve.

Chapter One

From Wynne's Journal:

My name is Wynne Ignitus. I don't know why I'm writing this down, other than my conscience will no longer allow me to turn a blind eye to what has been done, is being done, and my part in it. When our fuel was running out and we reached this world the humans living here thought we were nothing but another colony ship. Little did they know we were fugitives, fleeing the Ardraci authorities. It's been the perfect refuge. Who would think to look for Dr. Arjun and his followers on an agricultural world? The most brilliant scientist in the galaxy on a world that eschews the use of technology, a world where we are forced to hide what we do behind the walls of this immense compound. We've been here for more than a year and there is no sign of the other ships. There were five altogether, we're the only one that made it this far. Dr. Arjun has continued his experiments, but how can his breeding program still be viable with so small a gene pool to work from? But he is a man obsessed, de-

termined to create the perfect Elemental. There are times when I wonder if he is still sane.

Rayne stopped and looked around. Trees towered above her, smaller trees and shrubs filling in the spaces between, making it seem darker than it really was. This part of the forest looked the same as all the rest, which made it as good a place as any to pass the night. She eased the pack off her shoulders and let it drop to the ground, arching her back to ease the ache.

If she had a choice, she wouldn't stop at all, but it was too dangerous to go on in the dark. As it was, she could barely see the faint path she'd been following. She needed to rest, and she needed to gather wood for a fire while it was still light enough to see. It was cold on the mountain and was only going to get colder. This was a poor time of year to be attempting this, but that was one of the reasons she must.

This would make her third night spent on the mountain. Time was growing short, this was taking far too long but what did she know of woodcraft? It was just dumb luck she was still alive. A reasonable person would turn back, but any time she even considered it her sister's face came to mind and her resolve strengthened. Failure was not an option, she had to succeed.

The cold woke her at sunrise. Her fire was just about out and it was snowing. Under other circumstances she would have enjoyed the fat, fluffy flakes, but out here, alone, it was a different matter.

Cursing under her breath she kicked dirt over the remains of her fire and packed up as quickly as possible, not even taking time to eat first. She had to hurry before the snow covered what few landmarks she knew to look for. If she didn't find him today, she wouldn't find him at all.

* * * * *

Pyre watched from the protection of the trees. He'd been following the woman for two days now, curiosity getting the better of him. Though he knew what she was looking for, he didn't know why, and it was the why that made him curious. It had been a long time since someone had come to his mountain.

He shook his head as she packed up her camp without stopping to eat. She was a fool if she thought she'd last the day without something to sustain her. The cold had already sapped her strength, she needed fuel for her body.

At first he'd thought she was lost and had been fully prepared to reveal himself long enough to put her on the correct path back to the village. The longer he watched her, however, the more he realized she had a destination in mind. It wasn't until late in the second day that he realized what her destination was.

She was totally unsuited for the woods, even more so than he'd been in the beginning. It was only luck that she hadn't run into a bear, and even luckier it was still too early to worry about wolves. There was a part of him that couldn't help but admire her tenacity. What could she possibly be running away from that would send her up his mountain?

He was alone by choice and by necessity. The woman's presence disturbed his hard won peace of mind. He would watch, and wait. Perhaps he would find a chance to nudge her back towards the village. Perhaps the snow would take her and solve the problem for him.

* * * * *

Rayne thought of nothing more than putting one foot in front of the other. She had to keep moving, if she stopped she'd freeze to death and no one would find her body until the spring thaw, and that's assuming she was still on the trail.

A shape loomed up out of the swirling snow. At first she thought it was a tree and side-stepped to go around it, but when she looked up again it was still in front of her. She frowned in confusion. This was not a tree, it was a man. Was it the man she was looking for?

Too late. She no longer had the strength to find out. Her eyes closed and she sank to the ground.

Pyre looked down at the woman lying at his feet. Even exhausted and covered in snow she was beautiful. She was going to be nothing but trouble. With a sigh he picked her up and began the journey to his cave.

* * * * *

Rayne stirred, waking slowly. She sighed and snuggled down into the warmth of the furs, she'd never felt anything so luxurious in her life. All at once her eyes snapped open. She was in an unfamiliar bed and the softness of the fur was felt against her bare skin. Clutching the fur to her she sat up quickly.

"Where—" She was in a cave, lit by the comforting glow of a fire. Rising from the far side of the fire was a strange man. "Who—" Shock stole her voice. Whoever the man was, he was beautiful. He was tall and lithe, though he appeared well-muscled, with dark auburn hair flowing down almost to his waist. His face was finely sculpted and his eyes seemed to reflect the light of the fire.

Silently they stared at each other.

"You rescued me from the storm," she said finally. It was a statement, not a question.

He nodded once, then gestured to where her clothing was draped on some kind of drying rack beside the fire, answering her unspoken question. "Your garments were wet, it was necessary to remove them so you did not become ill."

She swallowed hard, imagining those large, elegant hands touching her as he undressed her.

"I—are you Pyrphoros?"

His features hardened. "Pyrphoros is no more. I am only Pyre now. Why were you on my mountain?"

"Your mountain?" She quirked an eyebrow at him.

He stood unmoving, staring at her. She'd been warned he was reticent, maybe even difficult, but she hadn't believed he'd truly be so unfriendly. This was not going to be easy.

She looked around curiously. There wasn't much to see. The fire pit was in the centre of the chamber, a rough hewn table and chairs set to one side. The opposite side had a cupboard of sorts and next to it was a pile of more furs. A chair, draped in yet another fur, rested near the fire, an open book lying face down on it.

Absently, she stroked the fur with her free hand. She was lying on a small fortune's worth of pelts. "Did you trap all these animals yourself?" she asked.

Her question was met with a stony silence. With a sigh she answered his question before asking any more of her own.

"I was looking for you."

"Why?"

"I need your help," she said, hoping her honesty might make a difference.

"You don't want my help," he said, turning away.

"Wait!" Cursing under her breath she clutched the furs to herself and tried to follow, but the darkness beyond the fire swallowed him up.

With a sigh she settled back on the bed. No, this wasn't going to be easy in the least.

Pyre moved quickly down the passage and out into the night air. It was still snowing; he was surprised the flakes didn't hiss as they touched him. He had to get himself under control. This was the very reason why he lived apart.

The woman was even more breath-taking awake; sitting up in his bed all sleepy-eyed, her pale hair tumbling loose around her bare shoulders. She made him yearn for impossible things.

She'd been wet from the snow and half-frozen by the time he'd gotten her to the cave. Her body temperature was dangerously low and he'd had no other choice but to warm her using the heat from his own body. He could still feel the silkiness of her skin next to his, it was a sensation he would not soon forget.

His steps slowed and then stopped. He took a deep breath of the night air and looked up at the stars, wishing that things could have been different. With a sigh he turned and slowly retraced his steps.

Wishing was for fools, he'd learned that a long time ago.

It didn't matter why she was looking for him. He had a good idea who'd sent her and that person, above all, should have known better. No, the sooner he got rid of her the better for everyone. They'd leave at first light.

Chapter Two

From Wynne's Journal:

There is still no trace of the other ships. Dr. Arjun chafes at the time it takes for the children of his experiments to mature enough to be used themselves. We have twelve maturation chambers, but even so the child must be no younger than two, no older than five when they enter it. And it still takes another year inside before their bodies have matured to the point where they are useful. He's started spending copious amounts of time in the secured lab with only his most trusted assistants for company. No one talks about what goes on behind that sealed door, but you can almost taste the fear.

With relief he saw the woman was dressed again when he returned to the cave, her pale hair pulled back from her face. She was sitting on the ground near the fire but looked up with a gasp as he appeared out of the darkness.

"You should get some rest," he said gruffly, gesturing towards the sleeping platform. "We leave at first light."

"Leave?" she said, scrambling to her feet. "Both of us?"

Her reaction confused him. She said she'd been looking for him, but after all she went through to find him, she seemed relieved to be leaving again. He was almost sorry she'd given up so easily, and that in turn annoyed him.

"I will guide you to the lower trail, you'll be able to find the rest of the way to the village from there."

"No! Please, you need to come back to the village with me."

Pyre shook his head. "I need do no such thing."

"Please," she took a step towards him, reaching out with her hand. Her hand dropped as he backed out of her reach. "Just listen to what I have to say."

He made the mistake of looking into her eyes. They were large in her elfin face, pale blue with a thick fringe of lashes, full of emotion that he was unable to keep himself distant from.

"All right," he agreed. "I'll listen to what you have to say. But don't expect me to change my mind." He gestured to the table. "We might as well sit down while you explain yourself."

Her relief was palpable. She slid into the chair and rested her hands on the table. Once he was seated opposite her, she hesitated, as though unsure of where to start.

"My name is Rayne," she began.

"That would make you a Water Elemental, would it not?"

She grimaced. "Yes. Those who named us had a singular lack of imagination."

"All right, Rayne, why do you need me to go with you to the village?"

"It's not for me, it's for my sister."

He raised an eyebrow but made no comment.

"Like you, her gift is fire, and the time of *tespiro* is almost upon her."

Pyre frowned. "What has this to do with me?"

"We ran out of the drugs that make the transition easier more than two years ago. Without the drugs, those entering *tespiro* have no control. They need someone of their element to guide them through the transition. There are no other Fire Elementals in the village."

"My presence would help no one." Bitterness laced his tone, memories came surging back and he fought for control.

"I've seen the difference it can make. Please! We have no way of knowing how strong her gift is until she undergoes the *tespiro*," Rayne faltered. "I have heard of what can happen to a Fire Elemental at this time. I do not want to lose my sister!"

"Find another," he said. "You do not know what you're asking of me."

"There is no other!"

He started to shake his head in denial, the dark memories he had locked away threatening to spill over.

"Please." Before he could stop her she left her chair and knelt at his feet. "I will do anything, anything you wish if you will come with me."

He grabbed her by the shoulders and pulled her up until they were face to face. "Do you have any idea what you are offering?"

"I know exactly what I'm offering," she said breathlessly. She couldn't look away from his eyes, they were filled with flames and it was not from the fire behind them. "I would do anything to save my sister."

He glared at her and then suddenly his lips came down on hers, hot and hard. Rayne felt her own element stir, brought to the surface by the intimate contact. Fire and water should not have been compatible, but this felt so very right. She pressed closer as he warmed all the cold places inside her.

As suddenly as he started kissing her, Pyre was pushing her away. "No, I can't do this."

Rayne stared up at him, wide-eyed.

"I'm sorry, I didn't mean—" he stared down at her, jaw clenched.

"You didn't mean to do that? It certainly felt like you meant it." She was hurt and confused. He had to have felt the connection between them, how could he just dismiss it? "It's me, isn't it? It's me you don't want."

He flushed and abruptly turned away. "You don't understand."

She put a hand on his arm to stop him from leaving. "You're right, I don't understand. You need to explain it to me."

"I can't." He tried to pull away but her hand tightened.

"Pyrphoros, please talk to me."

The urge to unburden himself was strong, and growing stronger every moment he was near her. This woman was making him weak and he couldn't afford to be weakened.

"The last woman I was with is dead by my hand," he said harshly. "Does that sound like someone you wish to be the savior of your sister?" He jerked his arm out of her grasp left her sitting alone.

Rayne was too shocked to protest. He was a murderer? She couldn't have heard right. The Mother would have never sent her to bring a murderer back to the village. There must be another explanation.

The temperature around her had dropped without the heat of his presence. She moved back over to her seat near the fire, trying to remember everything the Mother had told her of Pyrphoros. To be honest, she hadn't really paid close attention at the time. All she cared about was that there was someone with a strong enough gift to help her sister. Now she wondered if she'd missed an important detail.

"He has been too long alone," the Mother told her. "He cannot hide forever, he needs to return to us."

"Who is he hiding from?" Rayne had asked.

"From himself, from the past, from things that cannot be changed, only dealt with."

"But he can help Tanwen?"

"If anyone can ease her through the *tespiro* it is he." The Mother regarded her thoughtfully. "Though you differ in elements, you and he would do well together."

"You know I have problems in that area," Rayne said, flushing.

The Mother smiled. "You have both been wounded by the past; perhaps you can help each other heal."

Rayne doubted it and told the Mother so. There had been more to the conversation, something about a secret and a secret to be shared . . . She sighed and tried to relax. "From the looks of things, I guess I won't be figuring it out any time soon."

"Won't be figuring out what?"

She gasped as Pyrphoros' voice came out of the darkness. He hadn't left, only withdrawn into the shadows. "I didn't realize I'd spoken aloud."

"When it is light out I will take you back to the village. I will speak with the Mother to see if there is truly anything I can do to help your sister."

Unaccountably, her eyes filled with tears. "Thank you, I—"

"Do not thank me." His voice was colder than the air around her.

"Pyrphoros —"

"It's Pyre."

"I beg your pardon?"

"My name is Pyre." He laid a bedroll down on his side of the fire. "Get some sleep, there are only a few hours until dawn. The bed is yours."

"What about you?" she asked, scrambling to her feet.

"I'll be fine over here. I have my fire to keep me warm."

Rayne opened her mouth to protest and then closed it again. There were so many questions she wanted to ask him but they would have to wait until morning. She doubted she'd get any more out of him tonight. She was suddenly tired, both physically and emotionally; too tired to argue with him.

Pyre kept his back to the woman, busying himself with the bedroll. In a moment he heard light foot-steps and the creak of the bed. The tension began to slowly drift out of him. He meant what he said, that he would help her sister if at all possible. Perhaps it would in some small way redeem him. The Mother knew, better than anyone, what he was capable of.

Chapter Three

From Wynne's Journal:

I have a secret, a secret so great I fear almost to set it down here. I have a talent that no one knows of. As well as my small gift for fire, I can sense things before they happen - sometimes I have visions of the future. They have grown stronger since we've settled on this world, and lately they have focused on one person in particular – Ardralla. Her parents were both Fire Elementals, as she is, which should not matter but somehow it does. They were part of the program and had been altered genetically before Ardralla was conceived. Her tespiro, the time an Elemental comes into their power, was violent, indicating the strength of her gift. Since that time Dr. Arjun has kept her close, which is why she was on his ship instead of the one her parents were on when we fled the home world. Now, as she approaches the age he has set for optimum breeding my feeling of expectancy grows. It is not a sense of foreboding I feel, more a prelude of some momentous event.

Pyre was awake with the dawn. He had slept only fitfully, too aware of the woman in his bed, too haunted by nightmares. With his mind he stirred up the fire, helping ignite the wet wood he'd added. Glancing over, he saw the woman curled up in the very centre of the bed, still sound asleep.

Gathering up a change of clothing, he padded silently past her towards the back of the cave. Torches flared to life as he moved into the passage that led to a hot spring. Steam wafted gently through the air as he stripped off his clothing and slid into the water.

With a sigh he relaxed, allowing himself to be soothed by the hot water. He tried to clear his mind but visions of the woman kept intruding, of her soft, flawless skin, her pale blue eyes, and her full, luscious lips. The water heated around him.

With a curse he finished up and dressed in fresh clothing. The sooner they left for the village, the better. He would talk to the Mother, visit his foster-mother, and then return here alone, as it was meant to be.

He returned to the main chamber of the cave and stood near the bed, watching the woman silently for a moment. What was it about her? Her presence was like a balm to his soul, but he could not afford to be soothed, not if he were to survive.

Reaching down, he shook her shoulder gently, withdrawing his hand again the instant she stirred.

"It is morning," he told her. "We should be leaving soon."

Rayne stretched, cat-like. Pyre's eyes heated and he quickly turned away.

"There is a hot spring at the end of that passage," he said, nodding towards the tunnel. "If you wish to wash up you may do so in privacy."

"Thank you," she said quietly.

He waited for her to say something else, she seemed always to have more to say, but she merely gathered her things and disappeared down the passage.

The passageway was lit with torches held in sconces set in the walls. The chamber at the end of the passage was much smaller than the main cave, and the hot spring bubbled up in the centre. It was large, with a raised edge of mineral deposits around it. The heat from the water warmed the whole chamber by several degrees.

There was a neatly folded towel and a bar of soap beside the hot spring. Rayne smiled faintly, holding the soap to her nose. It was scented with wild flowers. She had no worries about privacy; he'd made it abundantly clear he wanted nothing to do with her, which was a shame. This pool was more than big enough for two.

The water was a little warm for her liking, but it still felt wonderful. She would have loved to have a nice long soak, but she wanted to get Pyrphoros back to the village before he changed his mind.

When she returned to the main cave, clean and dressed, Pyre was just finishing setting the table.

"I've made us breakfast," he said. "We need to eat before we leave, to sustain us."

It was like he needed an excuse to do something nice, she thought. What had happened that sent him so far up the mountain away from everyone? She didn't for a moment believe he murdered anyone, at least not intentionally. The Mother was right about one thing, Pyrphoros had been alone too long.

They ate in silence, each wrapped in their own thoughts. When they were finished, Pyre got rid of their dishes and Rayne retrieved her pack. When she turned back to him, he was holding out a bundle of furs to her.

"Here," he said gruffly.

She took the bundle and looked up at him, dumbfounded. "For me?"

"It's better suited to the cold than the coat you are wearing. There are leggings as well."

"I can't accept this," she said, stroking the soft fur. "It's too valuable."

"Accept it or not, it is your choice. Your clothing is inadequate and I have no wish to carry your frozen body back to the village."

He turned away and started pulling on his own set of furs. Rayne smothered a smile. If he thought his gruff attitude was fooling her, he was sadly mistaken. He was not nearly the monster he pretended to be.

She quickly pulled on the supple furs and followed him to the mouth of the cave. There she stopped in surprise, staring out at the brightness. "This isn't natural!" she blurted.

"No, it's not," Pyre agreed.

It had snowed steadily over night, covering the forest with a thick blanket of white. Snow was far from unusual on the mountain, but rarely so early, and never in such quantity.

"I don't understand," Rayne whispered.

"Nor do I," Pyre admitted. He glanced down at her and tried to be reassuring. "It looks to me like someone's element got away from them. I'm sure there's a reasonable explanation but we won't know until we get to the village."

She shot him a look that told him she wasn't reassured at all, but followed as he led the way into the forest.

They travelled steadily, Pyre breaking the trail and Rayne following carefully in his footsteps. They stopped briefly at mid-day for a quick bite to eat, dried rations that Pyre had carried under his coat to keep from freezing.

The snow seemed to get thicker the further down the mountain they went, which made no sense, and it was getting colder. Rayne was more grateful than ever for his gift of the furs. Though her own clothing had been adequate when she left the village, she would not have made it far in this bitter cold.

It was still light out when Pyre stopped. Rayne was so intent on following in his footsteps that she nearly walked into him.

"What is it?"

"We should make camp for the night," Pyre told her, letting his pack drop to the ground.

"There are still a couple of hours of daylight left, shouldn't we keep going?" she asked.

He could see how tired she was and couldn't help but admire her willingness to push herself. "The next decent site is too far away. We'd never make it before full dark."

Part of her was happy to take his word for it, even following in his footsteps it had been hard going through the snow, but another part of her was fired with the need to get back to the village. Something was terribly wrong, she could feel it.

They passed the night beneath an overhang in a sheltering curve of rocks that had tumbled down from the ridge above. Pyre used his axe to strip away the lower branches of a fir tree to insulate them from the cold ground and was able to get a small fire going using his gift.

"You feel it too, don't you?" Rayne asked in the morning. She'd been so tired she'd had no trouble sleeping, despite the cramped sleeping space. In fact, she'd felt oddly comforted by his presence beside her through the night.

Pyre had been gazing off into the distance, towards the village. He didn't need to ask what she was talking about. "I feel . . . something." He finished cooking their breakfast and handed her a steaming bowl.

"Eat up. We should be able to reach the village before sunset."

"What is this?" she asked, looking at the contents dubiously.

He almost smiled at her expression. "It's grain stewed with berries, it tastes better than it looks. Trust me."

She looked at him with her pale blue eyes. "I wouldn't be here with you now if I didn't."

Chapter Four

From Wynne's Journal:

I fear for Ardralla. Dr. Arjun is obsessed with her, and not just because she's a Fire Elemental, like him. Even on Ardraci they're rare. Ardralla is one of only two female fire wielders we have with us. He did something to enhance her element before he impregnated her. I've tried to tell him that she's too young and too small — it will be a miracle if she carries a child to term and an even bigger one if she delivers safely, but he will not listen. He calls her his "wife" and guards her jealously. She's little more than a child herself and yet she carries his child within her. My gift, such as it is, is also fire and I have been assigned to attend her. I want no part of this, but what else am I to do? If I had the means I would contact the home world, or even the Ilezie, for help. But we are alone, and I fear for the offspring of this madness. I fear for us all.

The uneasiness they'd been feeling worsened as the day progressed. The closer they got to the village, the deeper the snow became, which validated their theory the snow originated from there.

They were still a few miles from the village when Pyre stopped.

"Why are we stopping?" Rayne asked.

"Do you smell that?"

She took several deep breaths through her nose and then paled. "Is that—?"

"Smoke."

"No!" Rayne moaned and fell to her knees.

Pyre crouched down beside her. "You don't know that has anything to do with your sister. Even if she began her *tespiro* the day you left it would be too soon for her element to manifest."

She looked at him with tear-filled eyes. "How do you know?"

"I don't, for sure." He couldn't lie to her, even to reassure her. "But it took me almost a week before I could even light a candle."

"Truly?"

"Truly." He didn't go on to tell her the rest. That after his gift began to manifest the Mother had taken him to a cave to care for him to keep him from burning down the entire village. He helped her to her feet. "It's just like the snow, we won't know anything for sure until we reach the village."

Rayne sniffled and wiped her eyes. "You're right. I'm sorry. I—"

"Don't be. I don't have any siblings, but my foster-mother is still in the village."

"Thank you," she said quietly.

When he looked at her in surprise she continued, "For being here with me. I don't think I could have faced this alone."

Pyre was caught off guard by a surge of emotion. He was glad he was with her too, which made no sense at all. He was a loner, he preferred his own company to that of others. Why did she have this affect on him?

"Come on," he said gruffly. "We need to get to the village before nightfall."

With a sigh she fell into step behind him again. They'd gone only a short distance before she became aware that although the snow around them was heavier, she was not having as much trouble on the path. She glanced down, puzzled, then at the man in front of her.

The snow was almost gone from the path. Pyre was somehow using his gift to clear it away. The big question was, was he doing deliberately, or was he doing it subconsciously? A smile curved her lips. It didn't really matter.

The smell of smoke worsened as they neared the village. It was really just a cluster of houses and shops around a village green. Though some might consider it a haphazard layout, one of the reasons the settlers first came to this world was to get away from regimented order. Pyre and Rayne could see very little through the trees, which didn't make things any easier when the trees thinned and they got their first good look at the destruction.

Rayne whimpered in the back of her throat and Pyre put his arm around her without even being aware of it. A few of the houses on the edge of the village looked like they'd been blown to pieces; most of the rest were in various degrees of smouldering.

"I don't suppose I could persuade you to wait here while I check things out?" Pyre asked.

She shook her head, unable to speak. The fear of what might have happened to her family warred with her desire to run back up the mountain and not stop until she was back in Pyre's cave. When he felt her begin to tremble, his arm tightened around her shoulders.

"I'm all right," she said after a few moments, a determined lift to her chin. "Let's get this over with."

His arm slipped from her shoulders, but he took her hand as they stepped forward. The first house they reached had a corner of the roof missing and scorch marks on the front of it.

"That's Demetra and Eunan's home," Rayne whispered.

"Stay here," Pyre told her in a voice that brooked no argument.

She didn't know which was worse, staying out here by herself or imagining what was in the house. Her imagination barely had time to start working before he was back again.

"There was no one there," he said. "It's empty."

She tried to come up a reasonable explanation for them not being here, putting their house to rights again. "They must be helping with the fires that are still going."

"I don't know, but those scorch marks aren't the work of a Fire Elemental."

"They're not?" Rayne stared at him blankly. "But what else could have started these fires?"

"A weapon," he said grimly. "Many weapons."

While she tried to wrap her mind around the idea of a weapon that could cause such destruction, they continued onwards, moving slowly and cautiously. They checked two other houses but both were as empty as the first. It was not until they were nearly at the village square that they found the first body.

"That's Heddy, I recognize her shawl," Rayne said. "She's teaching me to weave."

Pyre knelt down beside the body and gingerly rolled it over. He didn't need to check for a pulse to know she was dead, the burn mark from the blaster said it all.

"Who could have done this?" Rayne asked, tears in her eyes.

"I don't know. It doesn't make any sense."

"Do you think they're all—" she swallowed and tried again. "Do you think there are survivors?"

He hesitated only a moment before shaking his head. "I don't know," he repeated, frustration leaking into his voice. He sat back on his heels and looked around them. The utter silence was disconcerting. "If it was a raid of some kind it's possible that some of the survivors might have made it to the forest."

Standing up he dusted the snow off himself. He took several steps forward before he realized she wasn't following. Pyre turned to face her. "What is it?"

"We can't just leave her here."

"What would you have me do?" He spread his hands wide.

She stared at him in mute appeal. He glanced at the body and sighed. "The ground's too frozen to bury her, what if I put her inside one of these buildings?"

Rayne nodded. "That one," she pointed. "It doesn't look as . . . damaged."

Carefully, he picked up the cold body and carried it into the building. It appeared to be some kind of feed store. He looked around for some place to put her and Rayne brushed past him to clear off the counter at the back.

He laid the body down and stood back to give Rayne a moment to say goodbye to her friend. After a few minutes he touched her gently on the shoulder.

"We need to get going."

She nodded and followed him back outside.

"Which direction is your home?"

Her eyes were wide and haunted. "It's on the other side of the square."

"Maybe you should stay here while I check on ahead," he suggested, looking towards the village square.

Rayne bit her lip, but moved up beside him. "I have to face it sooner or later," she said. "Let's get this over with."

Pyre's hand unerringly found hers and he squeezed it slightly before leading her forward. They passed more scorched and charred buildings but didn't see any more bodies. At least not until they came within viewing distance of the village square.

Rayne cried out and turned to bury her face in Pyre's chest. He held on to her tightly, staring word-lessly at the carnage. It looked as though the villagers had gathered in the square and then someone opened fire on them. Some of them tried to get away, there were individual bodies sprawled in the streets, but most of them had fallen where they stood.

"Why?" he asked. It made no sense. None of it did. There was little of value in the village, certainly nothing worth killing over. His eyes narrowed as he stared at the slaughter.

"We need to keep looking."

"What for?" Rayne pulled away slightly. "Haven't we seen enough?"

"They aren't all here."

She looked up at him wordlessly then, steeling herself, turned and looked at the bodies herself. Fresh tears ran down her face. These people were her friends, her family was probably lying there somewhere. She sniffed and wiped her tears away, taking a closer look.

"The Gifted," she said. "Those who are Gifted are missing."

Chapter Five

From Wynne's Journal:

Four months into her pregnancy, I started to suspect Ard-ralla's control of her element was slipping. She tried to hide it, but I saw the scorch marks and smelled the smoke. Once Dr. Arjun stopped by while I was with her and I swear I saw flames between the fingers of her clenched hands. At first he was oblivious to anything but her physical health and the health of their child, but even he could no longer turn a blind eye when she stopped talking. Although she eats when I bring her a tray, and comes with me obediently when I suggest we take a walk for exercise, she shows no emotion. There is a vacant look in her eyes and her smile is that of a child. Dr. Arjun has put a twenty-four hour watch on her, as though he fears she will harm either herself or her babe. At this point, I honestly don't know which one his concern is for. May the gods damn him for what he has done.

Pyre pulled an unresisting Rayne away from the village square. The shadows were growing longer, it was going to be dark soon. They needed to find some place to pass the night. Not that he expected either of them to get much sleep.

He stopped suddenly. "What about the Mother?"

Rayne made a visible effort to pull herself together. "The Mother? Do you think she might have escaped?"

"They might not have even known she was there."

"Yes, the Mother. We have to go to her!" She tore away from his grip and started to run.

"Rayne, wait!" Cursing under his breath he hurried after her. There was no telling what might be waiting for them in the Mother's home. Though Rayne had done well up to this point he didn't think she could take any more shocks. If anything had happened to the Mother . . .

The Mother's home was set apart from the village, deeper in the forest. Pyre caught up to Rayne just outside the Mother's door. The cottage didn't appear to be damaged, there were no scorch marks marring the weathered wood, but there was no smoke coming from the stone chimney and no light coming from within.

"I'm afraid," she admitted.

"I'll go first," Pyre told her.

"No," she shook her head. "We'll go in together."

Buoyed by the strength of his presence, she opened the door and stepped across the threshold. They paused a moment to allow their eyes to adjust to the dimness. Pyre went over to the fireplace to build a fire and Rayne moved slowly towards the corner of the room that held the Mother's bed. She stood looking down at the slight figure lying under the blankets and then knelt down beside the bed. Reaching out, she smoothed the hair away from the wrinkled face and then rested two fingers against the artery in the Mother's neck.

"Is she . . ." Pyre came over to stand beside her.

"No, she's alive, but she's very weak." She looked up at him. "She was ill before I left, but she insisted I find you. Someone else was supposed to stay with her while I was gone."

"I sent them away," the Mother whispered. "If I hadn't, they might have been saved."

"Mother," Pyre hunkered down beside Rayne. "Can you tell us what happened?"

"It was the thing I feared all these years."

"Don't try to talk," Rayne said, shooting Pyre a fierce look. "You need to save your strength. When was the last time you ate?"

"No child," the Mother said in her whispery voice. "My time is nearly at an end. It falls to the two of you to make things right."

"Make things right? What are you talking about?"

"He's taken the children, you must save them."

"She means the Gifted," Rayne whispered.

"Who's taken the children?" Pyre asked.

"And how can we save anyone, we are just two against armed raiders," Rayne added.

"You will seek help. There is a book on the mantel. You must go to the spaceport and contact the Ilezie. Give them the book. They will know what to do."

"The spaceport? You told me to never go there, not even to trade my furs," Pyre said.

"Secrecy is no longer a priority. Rescuing the children is. The burden I once shouldered alone is now yours to share."

Rayne and Pyre looked at each other. "Mother, we don't understand," said Rayne.

"You will, in time. There, in my trunk, you'll find all the currency you'll need for your journey. There's a letter with instructions as well."

"We're not leaving you here," Rayne said stubbornly.

"You won't have a choice, child. Now, I need to speak with Pyrphoros a moment. Perhaps you could fetch in some more firewood."

Rayne looked decidedly unhappy as she went outside to find the woodpile.

"She is far more powerful than she knows," the Mother said to Pyre. "He can't be allowed to discover her true gift."

"He? Who is this mysterious he? And is he the one responsible for what happened to the village?"

"He is a powerful enemy. Never forget that. Never forget what he's done to our village." She paused to cough.

"Can I get you something to drink?"

"No, I'm fine," she waved him off. "I need a promise from you."

"What promise?"

"That if you two are captured, you will take Rayne's life."

Pyre couldn't believe he heard her right. "Mother, I—"

"Promise me!" she said fiercely. She reached up to him. Her hand was white and wasted, but she gripped his arm with a manic strength.

"I cannot. You don't know what you're asking." He shook his head in denial.

"Yes I do. Already you share a bond with her that will only deepen with time—"

He tried to pull away but she only tightened her grip.

"There is no shame in what you feel. She is not like Angana – what happened is not your fault!"

The air around them began to heat. Pyre's eyes glowed in his pale face and the Mother matched him glare for glare.

All at once the fierceness seemed to drain from her and she released his arm with a sigh. "Your foster mother was right, I should never have let you go off alone."

"You couldn't have stopped me," he said, rubbing his arm.

"Oh, I could have if I'd felt it necessary, never doubt that boy."

Pyre looked at the frail old woman lying weighted down by the quilts on her bed and didn't doubt it for a moment. This was the Mother, the village leader, their wise woman, and their healer. The Mother was the heart of the village.

"Now, about that promise . . ."

"You cannot ask such a thing of me! To take a life—"

"Will be the greatest kindness you could do for her should she fall into his hands. You have no idea of the cruelties he is capable of." A shudder went through her. "It's not like I'm asking you to go out and slit her throat right now, all I ask is that should the unthinkable happen you take a life to save a soul."

Pyre could not conceive of anything so terrible that would warrant the taking of an innocent life. What could this unknown enemy do that could threaten someone's very soul? "I will promise to think on it," he said. "And should the need arise I will do what I believe is right."

"I suppose it is the best I can hope for," the Mother said grudgingly. "Now go send Rayne in to me. The poor child is probably half frozen out there. I need to talk with her as well."

Rayne was sitting on a stump in the Mother's yard, a small pile of wood at her feet, when Pyre opened the door. One look at his expression was enough to stop her questions. He looked shaken and kept his gaze averted from her.

"She wants to see you," he said, then left the cottage and moved quickly away, back towards the village.

She took a step in the direction he'd taken, wanting to offer comfort, then shook her head and resolutely went into the cottage.

"Come sit by me, child," the Mother told her.

"You should rest," Rayne told her. "You're still very weak from your illness. At least let me make you some broth."

"Perhaps later. Now sit."

Used to obeying the Mother, Rayne did as she was told. The Mother looked at her and sighed. "Such slender shoulders to carry such a burden," she said. "But it cannot be helped. I know the task I have set you and Pyrphoros is nigh unto impossible, but with the help of the Ilezie I have faith you will succeed in rescuing the children."

"Who are the Ilezie?"

"They are . . . the caretakers to our race. If only I had found the courage to contact them in the beginning then things might have turned out differently, but I was not thinking clearly back then."

Privately Rayne thought the Mother was not thinking clearly now. It was unlike her to ramble like this and it worried her.

"And if, with the help of these Ilezie, we are able to save the other Gifted, then what? Everyone else in the village . . ." here she faltered. "There's no one left."

For the first time the Mother looked uncertain, and that frightened Rayne more than anything else that had happened over the last few days.

"That will be up to the Ilezie," she said at last. "They are powerful, but part of that power is their sense of justice. They would never harm an innocent and the children are completely innocent of any wrong doing."

"But—"

"Enough. I have one more thing to tell you, and then I must rest."

"Surely it could wait—"

"No, it can not. It concerns you . . . and Pyrphoros."

Chapter Six

From Wynne's Journal:
It is done, and the only regret I have is that I could not save them both. Dr. Arjun was dealing with an emergency in the settlement when Ardralla went into labor. For the first time in weeks she was thinking clearly. It is she who has set me on the path. She asked that I see to it her child is not raised in the compound and though I did not know how I was to accomplish it, I agreed. The birth was even more horrifying than I'd imagined but Dr. Arjun's absence allowed me enough time to hide the child. Ardralla stayed with us until Dr. Arjun arrived, then let go of her element and went up in flames, letting him believe the child went with her. The death of Ardralla weighs heavily on me. I keep thinking there should have been something I could have done to prevent it but I know in my heart only Dr. Arjun could have prevented this tragedy. I have a plan, but I cannot do it alone. I believe there are those among us who think as I do, it is just a matter of finding them. In the

meantime, Ardralla's child thrives, a happy, healthy boy. I have found a foster mother for him among the humans. She knows of the hazards of keeping him, but she loves him like her own and that, at least, makes it worth the risk of discovery.

"Pyrphoros?" Rayne repeated.

"Yes," the Mother said firmly. "I have a story to tell. It is not mine—" she broke off and started to cough.

Rayne got a cup of water and held it so the Mother could sip from it.

"Perhaps this should wait until you're feeling better," Rayne suggested.

"No," the old woman was adamant. "I must speak. You children are not the same as other Elementals, many of you have special gifts."

"You mean like mine?"

The Mother smiled. "No, there is no one like you. You are unique. Now stop interrupting."

She motioned towards the cup and Rayne held it so she could take another sip of water.

"There was a girl whose gift was the ability to enhance the power of others. Used wisely it could have been of great benefit to us all . . . Unfortunately, she was twisted of spirit and mind, a fact we did not discover until it was too late." The Mother shook her head slightly.

"She would wait until a boy had entered his *tespiro* and then make advances to him. Of course what teenaged boy would turn down an offer from a beautiful girl? She would wait until they were about to become intimate and then suddenly enhance their power. The boys would be terrified that they were losing control of their element."

"Those poor boys!" Rayne said.

"Of course none of them spoke up about it; if we had known sooner . . . Two of the boys recovered, but three of them never got over their fear of intimacy."

"And Pyre is one of the three?" Rayne guessed.

"Ah, Pyrphoros. He's the one that put an end to her, and in doing so suffered the worst trauma of all. We had just discovered what she'd been doing when she got her hooks into him."

The Mother motioned for another sip of water. Rayne patiently held the cup for her, though she felt anything but patience for the end of the story.

"I suppose to be fair, none of us knew just how powerful Pyrphoros was to become. Perhaps if Angana, that was her name, knew she might have left him alone." The Mother shrugged slightly. "Perhaps not. Who's to know? In any case, Angana's preferred trysting place was an old barn on the edge of the village."

Rayne had a sinking feeling she knew where this was going.

"As you might guess, the barn was dry and filled with hay, and when Angana enhanced Pyrphoros's gift it went up like a rocket. The explosion knocked Pyrphoros out cold, which is just as well. Her screams as she burned to death were terrible to hear."

The mother paused, remembering. "It was hours before we were able to get close enough to the fire to put it out. By that time Pyrphoros was just coming to. He'd lost his clothes, of course, but because fire was his element the rest of him was unscathed."

"Poor Pyrphoros!" To awaken in the ruins of a burning barn, knowing that only your element had saved you, he must have been terrified.

"He was horrified at what he'd done—"

"But it wasn't his fault!"

"No, it wasn't. But we could not get him to believe us. He would not even believe one of the other boys who came forward. And so he exiled himself from the village, determined that no one else should ever suffer if he lost control of his element again."

"It wasn't his fault," Rayne repeated softly.

"No, it was not," the Mother said firmly. "But unfortunately, the damage has been done. He will never be able to be with someone in that way without fearing that he will lose control of his element."

"I am grateful you have told me this," Rayne said. "But I must ask myself, why? Is this to warn me not to grow too attached to him, that we can never truly be together?"

"Quite the opposite, child. I have told you this because I can see that you already care for him, and I hope that you might understand him better."

"I do care for him," Rayne said slowly. "And I think he could come to care for me, if he let himself. But now, more than ever, I think it is hopeless."

"Tut, child. Where there is love, there is a way. Now that you know his secret there is only one thing left for you to do."

Rayne looked at her.

"You must tell him your secret."

"No!" The word was out of Rayne's mouth before she could even think about it. She flushed ducked her head. "Forgive me, I didn't mean to raise my voice. It's just . . ."

The Mother looked at her shrewdly. "It's just that you've become so conditioned to keeping your secret the very thought of sharing it frightens you."

Rayne kept her head down, refusing to meet the Mother's eyes.

"You have every reason to fear, child." The Mother laid her head back with a sigh. "So many secrets, for so many years. Not just yours, for many people. We are a village of secrets."

Cautiously, Rayne raised her head. "There are others like me?"

"No, child. As I have said, you are unique amongst a village filled with unique Elementals, probably amongst Elementals anywhere. Were he ever to find you . . ."

"He? Who is he?"

"He is the devil himself."

Rayne bit her lip in frustration. There were times when the Mother's cryptic remarks made her want to scream.

"You and Pyrphoros can never be together unless he knows the truth about you."

A sudden thought struck Rayne. "You knew, didn't you?"

"Knew what?" the Mother asked evasively.

"You knew that Pyre and I would be attracted to each other. Is that why you sent me to him? Was Tanwen just an excuse?"

"I . . ."

Her eyes widened. "Did you know the village would be attacked?"

Among the Mother's many other talents was the ability to "see" into the future. It was not a reliable gift, and often her visions needed interpretation, but it never failed to warn the village when a threat was near. It had stood them in good stead over the years.

It was understood by even the smallest child of the village that outsiders must never learn of gifts so many of them had, that it was dangerous and could lead to serious trouble for all. Outsiders were rarely welcomed, and then only with the Mother's approval.

"I knew only that there was something dreadful approaching, not what form it would take. I never imagined it would be so terrible."

"Who attacked the village? Do you know where they've taken the Gifted?"

"I don't know, I don't know," the Mother shook her head, clearly agitated. Rayne was beyond caring.

"The snow came first, trapping everyone in the village; he has true Elementals and they've learned to work together. Water and Air, that's all you need for snow. Then I heard the blasters, a sound I thought I'd never hear again, and the screams. They were on foot, I know that much. I think the only reason they left me alive was because they didn't know about me."

Rayne tried to imagine what it must have been like for the Mother, alone and ill, listening to the sounds of destruction and helpless to do anything about it.

"It was so long ago, so long ago," the Mother said. "I was so young and idealistic. Not as pretty as you, but I did all right. He made me think I was special . . ."

There was a faraway look in the Mother's eye as she continued, "It turned out we were all special, but not for the reasons we thought. He picked only those with the sharpest minds, the strongest gifts. To this day I don't know why he chose me."

The Mother was hallucinating, Rayne realized with a start of alarm. Her mind had wandered into the past. Gently she reached out and laid a hand on the Mother's forehead. As she'd feared, the Mother was burning up with a fever.

Chapter Seven

From Wynne's Journal:

Things have been steadily deteriorating in the compound for some time now. Where before we were a tightly woven community with a common goal, now we are a place of secrets and locked doors. I am ever on the alert for the opportunity to rescue more children, but almost two years have passed and it is only recently I have been able to do so. This time it was the girl-child of a Water Elemental. Namir had given birth to twins three years ago, and although Dr. Arjun was pleased with the boy, he was less so with the girl. His tests showed she would only be average in her element, a fault in the maternal line. Though he has put Namir through a course of genetic manipulation, he is unhappy with the results, mainly because the child she now carries is another girl. She has begged me for help – she fears Dr. Arjun will not let another girl live unless she is powerful in her gift, and tests have shown this is not to be so. After their children reach the age of two, Breeders are no longer allowed contact with them. This is so nothing impedes them from being bred again. The life she sees stretching before her is not one she can bear and she does not intend to survive the birthing of her daughter. She begs only that I see to it her daughter survives.

Rayne was pacing back and forth in front of the fireplace when Pyre finally returned to the cottage.

"Where have you been?" She turned on him furiously. "You've been gone for hours!"

"I went back to the village. The bodies . . . I moved them into the Meeting Hall." He looked at her with haunted eyes and her anger drained away. "I didn't know what else to do with them."

"Oh, Pyrphoros!"

Tears pricked at her eyes and she put her arms around him. The fact that he returned her embrace instead of pushing her away told her just how much he'd been affected by his grisly task. His arms tightened minutely before he seemed to recall himself and loosen his grip again.

"How is she?" he asked, nodding towards the Mother.

Rayne was disappointed, but not surprised, when he shut down their emotional connection again.

"She is very ill. I cannot bring her fever down. When she wakens, it is only for a few minutes at a time and she is delirious."

He sighed and turned to pace in front of the fire. "Every moment we delay puts that much more distance between us and the raiders who did this."

"But—"

"I know, I know, we cannot leave her alone either."

"You cannot save the children on your own," the Mother said in a reedy voice. "Only the Ilezie can deal with this. You must give me your word you will do ask I asked."

Pyre went over to the bed and knelt down beside her. "I promise we will not abandon you."

"I do not matter!" she said fiercely. "Only the children do. This has all been for the children!" Her face was flushed but her eyes were clear.

"Mother—"

"I want your word that you will take the book to the Ilezie."

"Mother, I—"

"Your word!"

"You have my word that I will take the book to the Ilezie," he agreed reluctantly. "Whoever the Ilezie are."

The Mother visibly relaxed. "Good. Don't forget the letter or the credit strips in my trunk. Now come closer, both of you."

They did as she asked and she took them each by the hand. "Though I have loved all the children in my care, you two were the first and the most special.

Never forget that." She brought their hands together. "Take care of each other, and remember that it does not show weakness to draw upon each other for strength."

She closed her eyes and her hands went limp.

"Mother!" Rayne cried out, reaching for her. Pyre held her back and she struggled in his grip. "What are you doing? Let go of me!"

"Look!" he insisted.

She focused her attention on the Mother and stilled. "What's happening?"

The Mother's form was surrounded by a blue nimbus. The glow was faint at first but grew steadily brighter. Streaks of yellow and orange appeared in the nimbus.

"She was a Fire Elemental!" Pyre exclaimed.

Rayne's eyes widened as the glow continued to intensify and the streaks became tongues of flame. The fire was contained by the Mother's body at first but the bedding was beginning to catch.

"We need to get out of here!" Pyre pulled Rayne towards the door.

"Wait! What about the book and the letter?" Flames were already licking at the trunk at the foot of the bed.

"You get the book, I'll get the letter – I can handle the fire."

Rayne grabbed the book off the mantle and snatched up their packs where they lay on the hearth.

She staggered towards the door, the smoke already too thick to see clearly. Pyre reached out a steadying hand and they escaped into the night.

They watched from the edge of the clearing as the Mother's cottage was engulfed in flames. As with all elemental fires, this one burned hot and fast. The heavy snow coating the trees and ground kept it from spreading.

"All these years," Rayne whispered. "I never suspected she was Gifted." How many other secrets had the Mother been keeping?

"It will be day break in a few hours," Pyre said. "We should really try and get some rest. It's a long way to the spaceport."

She looked at him in surprise. "I thought you wanted to follow the raiders?"

"I gave my word. And in any case, the Mother was right. We cannot do this alone. We don't even know who our enemy is, let alone where to find them."

"She seemed afraid – I've never known the Mother to fear anything," Rayne mused.

"She's putting a great deal of faith in the abilities of these Ilezie . . . I wish we knew more about them."

"I wish we knew more about a great many things," Rayne said with a sigh. "Such as where we are to sleep for the remainder of the night."

Pyre turned to lead the way back down the path.

"Where are you going?"

"We can't stay here; there are plenty of empty buildings in the village, we just need to pick one."

Rayne refused to move. "I can't. I just . . . can't."

Pyre took in her tear-streaked face, the lines of fatigue settling in, and didn't try to argue. Instead he looked around and then started down a different path. "I think I know a place."

"Are you sure your element is not earth?" Rayne asked after he led her through the nearby woods to a small cave. "You seem to have a great fondness for caves."

He smiled faintly. "My friends and I used to play here when I was a boy. One of the shop keepers had thought to make a storage place of it, but abandoned the idea."

The cave was not nearly as large as Pyre's cave on the mountain, but it was large enough for them and their packs, and it had a dry, sandy floor. Rayne sank to the ground with a sigh.

"Here." He handed her a cake made of dried fruit mixed with grains. "You need to eat something before you fall asleep."

There was not enough room for a fire, but Pyre filled a pair of tin cups with snow and then used his internal fire to heat them to make tea. Rayne sipped hers gratefully, too tired to try and make conversation. When she was finished she stretched out and, using her pack as a pillow, promptly went to sleep.

For Pyre, sleep did not come as easily. He couldn't stop thinking about what had happened in the village, nor of the number of dead. The Mother once told him she'd never heard of anyone with a gift of fire as powerful as his. And what had he done with it? Hidden away up on his mountain instead of protecting the village. Perhaps if he'd been there no one would have died.

As he'd placed each body in the meeting hall, he silently apologized for running away, for not being in the village when it mattered. He'd been unable to shed any tears, not even when he placed his foster mother gently down on the floor of the hall.

Rayne whimpered in her sleep and he glanced down at her. She was so beautiful. And so courageous. It was not going to be easy to travel all the way to the spaceport with her and keep his hands to himself. He had never been drawn to another person the way he was drawn to her.

Unable to help himself, he reached down and moved a stray strand of hair from her face, stroking her cheek lightly before pulling away again. Was the Mother right? Did he and Rayne share a bond?

Again she made that sound of distress. Pyre stretched out on the floor beside her and tentatively put his arms around her. She sighed in her sleep, relaxing fully, and snuggled closer to him.

Fire and Water. They should clash, not be drawn together. Water quenched fire and fire dried up water.

It should not be possible. But at this moment, Pyre was ready to believe in the impossible.

Chapter Eight

From Wynne's Journal:

Rescuing Namir's child was easier than I thought it would be, although I feared for my life when I was stopped on my way out of the compound by one of the researchers. She, too, has become concerned about what is happening and when she saw me sneaking through the back passages, followed me. When she realized what I was doing she offered her assistance. She kept watch while I did what I had to do. I have kept in touch with the first foster-mother I found, and left the second child with her that she might find her a fitting home. When I returned to the compound the researcher was waiting for me, along with two nurses and a technician. They say there are others, but we must be careful. Dr. Arjun would not hesitate to destroy anyone who gets in his way, he's already proved that. We meet in secret and I act as a liaison with the humans who are sympathetic to our cause. It is well that Dr. Arjun dis-

counts the humans. They will be the key to our success, though it may take years.

The moment Pyre felt Rayne stir in the morning he eased away from her. By the time she was fully awake he was sitting up and searching through his pack for the last of the rations he'd brought with them.

"Did you sleep at all?" she asked, accepting the rations he passed to her.

"I got some sleep. I'll sleep better once we're away from this place," he admitted.

Her eyes searched his face while she nibbled on a piece of dried fruit. He still looked tired, but more than that he looked troubled about something. "What's wrong?"

"There's nothing wrong . . ."

She continued to stare at him and he began to fidget. Finally he sighed. "You're not going to like it."

"I don't like any of this, what's one more thing?"

"It's a long way to the space port . . ."

"I know that," Rayne said when his voice trailed off. "Are you worried that I'm not up to a trip that far? I'm stronger than I look."

"No, that's not it at all. I have no doubt we'll be able to reach the space port easily."

"But?" she asked when his voice trailed off again.

"But I only brought enough supplies from my cave to last until we reached the village. We've just eaten the last of them."

"Is that all?" she asked with relief. She'd been afraid he was going to tell her she'd only slow him down, and that she should remain here while he went on ahead to the space port. "We'll just—" She broke off what she was going to say and her eyes widened. "No, we can't!"

"We'll never make it if we aren't properly equipped."

Her sentimentality overrode her common sense. "We can't! It'll be like robbing graves!"

"There's no other choice," he told her. He didn't like the idea any better than she did, but they had to be practical. "We will take only what we need—"

"We can't just take what isn't ours!" It was too final, akin to admitting they were not coming back.

"Do you think anyone in that village would begrudge even the slightest crumb if they knew it was going towards an attempt to save their children?"

It was Rayne's turn to hesitate. "Well, no. Not when you put it like that," she admitted reluctantly.

"We do what we must to survive," he said gently.

For a moment she thought he was going to reach out to her, but the moment passed.

"Let's get this over with," she said, climbing to her feet. "I don't want to spend any more time in the village than I have to."

"Agreed."

The village seemed even more ghostly than before. The morning sun shone brightly, highlighting the scorch marks on the buildings. There was a steady drip, drip of melting snow. Without the Elementals to influence the weather, it was returning to normal.

The desolation was even more marked that it had been the previous day. There was no smoke coming from the smithy on the edge of the village. The market stalls were empty, as were the animal pens. There were not even any chickens wandering loose. Though Pyre wondered where the animals had gone, a quick glance at Rayne's white face kept him from saying anything.

With unspoken accord, they headed straight for the trade and supply shop. Moving as quickly as possible, they found what they needed for their journey – durable clothing, sturdy footwear, dried fruit and meat, lightweight, thermal blankets and, after a long hesitation, a weather-proof tarp.

"Is that everything?" Rayne asked.

"Not quite," Pyre said.

He went over to a display case near the back of the store and removed a pair of long knives in sheathes. Rayne opened her mouth to argue when he held one out to her, knives weren't going to do much against weapons such as the raiders had, but only shrugged and tucked it into her pack. As an afterthought, he picked out two carved walking sticks as well.

"I think that's it," he said. "Are you ready to go?"

Her eyes shone with unshed tears, but she nodded and followed him out the door. They walked around the village square, the recent carnage too fresh in their minds for them to cross over it. Rayne glanced at the Meeting Hall and stopped.

"What is it?"

"Why didn't they return to their elements, like the Mother did?"

"I don't know. Maybe because it only happens when an Elemental dies of natural causes."

She glanced at Pyre, then back at the Meeting Hall.

"Just how powerful is your gift?"

His mouth opened, then shut again. He felt like he'd aged a hundred years in the last few days. She knew what she was asking of him, but it was only right.

Leaving his pack with Rayne, he walked up to the Meeting Hall and placed both hands on the wall. Smoke wafted upwards; soon flames were licking at the wood. When the entire side of the building caught, he stepped back and rejoined Rayne.

As they stood side by side, watching the building go up in flames, Rayne spoke the Final Blessing.

"May the Fire cleanse you; may the Water rain down in sorrow; may the Earth cradle the shell you once wore; and may the Wind carry your soul to the Great Beyond."

* * * * *

The further from the village they traveled, the warmer it became. Knowing the unseasonable weather was due only to elemental influence, they'd left the heavy furs they'd been wearing behind, opting for clothing more suited to travelling light. Melting snow gave way to no snow at all until the countryside was the way it should be for this time of year. At midday they passed through a sun-dappled clearing and Pyre suggested they take a break. Rayne nodded and dropped her pack to the ground, sinking down to sit on a fallen log.

She felt numb. Her parents were dead, as was everyone else in the village. The Gifted were missing. They were leaving behind the only life she'd ever known. She knew about the spaceport, of course, and of the technological wonders that could be found there, but she'd never had any desire to see them for herself.

Pyre felt weary to his soul. Even with a gift as powerful as his, using it to start a fire as large as he had took a lot out of him. He'd always imagined learning how to control his gift and then some day returning to the village in triumph. That was never going to happen now.

"We should eat something," he said, more to break the silence between them than out of any real desire to eat.

Rayne shivered. "I can't. I don't think I could keep food down."

Though part of him agreed, another part of him knew they needed to keep their strength up. Using the tin cups and water from the water bottle, he made them each a strong cup of tea, generously sweetened with honey.

"Try to drink some of this," he urged. "Even if it's just a few sips."

She dutifully took a sip and tears filled her eyes.

Pyre looked at her, appalled. "I'm sorry, I can make you something else—"

"No," she shook her head. "It's not that. It's just . . . my mother used to take her tea with honey." The tears spilled over as she looked at him in anguish.

He cursed himself under his breath for his thoughtlessness, although how was he to have known? Taking the cup from her, he placed it on the ground and then moved closer to her on the log. She clung to him, crying in earnest now, and he was help-less to do anything but hold her, stroking her hair and whispering soothing nonsense.

When her tears ran out she didn't pull away and he was content to just sit there, holding her. They stayed that way for a long while, taking comfort from each other.

"I'm sorry," she said, head resting on his shoulder.

"For what?" he asked in surprise.

"For falling apart like that."

"I think you're entitled," he said, arms tightening slightly around her. "You've been through a lot, we both have."

She raised her head slightly to look up at him. "I'm sorry I made you set fire to the meeting house, you must be exhausted."

He looked down into her eyes and what he saw there made his chest tighten. "It was the right thing to do."

"Like this," she whispered.

"Like what?"

She raised her face up the few inches it took to be able to kiss him. At first it was a soft, hesitant brushing of her lips over his, but when he didn't pull back she grew bolder. Pyre froze. For an instant he thought of pushing her away, but only for an instant. As her hands slid upwards to anchor themselves in his hair he began kissing her back.

It wasn't enough. With a groan he pulled her onto his lap. Rayne pressed closer to him, cursing the layers of clothing between them. Her hands left his hair and found the fastenings to his jacket, shoving it open before going to work on her own. He seemed oblivious to what she was doing and she guided his hands with hers, sighing in satisfaction as they finally found her aching breasts.

She pressed forward into his touch, crying out softly as his thumbs brushed over the sensitive peaks. At the sound of her cry he seemed to suddenly realize what he was doing and looked at her with something akin to panic in his eyes.

"No!"

Chapter Nine

From Wynne's Journal:

Although the official mortality rate of the births has gone up slightly, Dr. Arjun does not appear to notice. With all the genetic manipulation he is doing, it is to be expected. We have been careful, oh so careful, to cover our tracks. I am the only one in the compound who knows who amongst the humans can be trusted and I limit my contact with them. We have developed a system that is working well but I cannot help thinking our time is growing short. We cannot keep this up forever, we must make plans to break free. For every child we are able to save, three more are left behind and of these a select few are removed to the secure lab. I still do not know what goes on in there, but I have my suspicions. Dr. Arjun frets at the amount of time it takes for his experiments; I think he is enhancing the growth rate of these children so they can be used in the breeding program. Two of the lab techs, not ones who are part of our movement, left in the night. We have no idea if they left on their own or if Dr. Arjun had something to do with their disappearance. I don't know how much more of this I can stand.

"We cannot do this!" He slid out from under her and sprang to his feet, chest heaving as he tried to gain back some semblance of control.

Rayne looked at him, too shocked for words. She turned away to fumble with the fastenings to her clothing, tears pricking at her eyes. The Mother had been wrong, whatever Pyrphoros may feel for her, it was obviously not the attraction she felt.

"Rayne, I'm sorry. I—"

She shook her head. "No, I am the one who is sorry. I should not have thrown myself at you like that. I—I—I was not myself."

He took a step towards her. "Rayne, look at me."

"We should really get going, it's a long way to the space port." She scrambled to her feet and shouldered her pack, keeping her face turned so he wouldn't see her tears.

"Rayne—" Pyre sighed in frustration as she nearly tripped over the log in her haste to get back to the trail.

He couldn't have made more a mess of things if he tried. He knew she was upset, he just didn't know what to do about it. Far from rejecting her, he was only trying to protect her. He already cared too much for her to risk having her die in flames.

With another sigh he picked up his pack and followed slowly in her wake. Maybe this was for the best. Maybe if she believed he didn't care then she'd stay away from him. Maybe he'd stop being so tempted by her. Maybe he was only fooling himself.

Rayne struggled to stay a few steps ahead of Pyre while she got her emotions under control. As her humiliation began to fade, it was replaced by embarrassment and then a growing anger.

Maybe her timing hadn't been the best, but it wasn't as though she was taking advantage of him. He kissed her back. He must feel something for her, if not emotionally then at least physically. So why, then, did he keep pushing her away?

Unbidden, the Mother's voice filled her mind. "He will never be able to be with someone without fearing that he will lose control of his element."

Rayne's steps slowly slightly. It was what every one of them feared, losing control of their element. Shame filled her. After what Pyre had been through it was no wonder he shied away from any physical contact. She almost stopped to apologize again when she remembered he didn't know the Mother had told her his story.

It was so frustrating! She knew she'd be safe with him, but how was she to convince him of it without letting him know she knew his past? *Tell him your secret,* the Mother's voice whispered in her mind.

She shivered. Her gift would allow them to be together, but her secret would have him turn from her in revulsion. No, there had to be another way.

The day wore on and she still had no answer to her dilemma. Pyre found them a sheltered spot just off the trail to stop for the night. Silently they spread out the bedrolls and gathered wood for a fire. Pyre made the evening meal for them and afterwards they sat watching the dancing flames, neither sure how to break the silence between them.

"Rayne, I——" Pyre hesitated. Taking a drink from his cup of tea he gathered his thoughts for another try.

All afternoon he tried to think of a way to make things right between them again. He cared for Rayne, more than was wise perhaps, and he couldn't let her think he didn't. She already knew he was a murderer, he'd told her that when they first met, but she deserved to know the whole story and then she'd understand why they couldn't be together.

"When I was younger, just after I went through my *tespiro*, there was . . . I was . . ." He turned to face the fire, unable to face her. "Her name was Angana. She was younger than me, but far more experienced. She could have had her pick of anyone – I never knew why she chose me, I was just proud she had."

"Pyre, I——"

"No, please. You need to hear this." He took a deep breath and continued. "We met in an old barn at the edge of the village. It was my first time with a woman. We . . . it was . . . I'm still not sure what happened, just that I lost complete control over my element. There was an explosion. When I regained consciousness the barn was gone. And so was Angana."

He seemed to huddle in on himself as he stared into the flames. It was almost as though he was afraid to face her. Rayne suddenly realized that he'd been afraid of the very thing she was, that she'd reject him once she knew the truth about him.

"Pyrphoros, there's something you should know. I—"

"Ho, the camp fire!" a voice called from the dark.

Pyre was on his feet in an instant, Rayne a little slower to rise. By the time the stranger was close enough to the fire that they could make out his form, they were standing side by side. From childhood they'd been taught to be wary of strangers, to never, under any circumstances, use their gifts around them. No matter how trustworthy a stranger might be, they'd been told, they would never understand an Elemental's gift.

The man who approached seemed harmless enough. He was of middle height, somewhat stocky, and had the weather-worn look of someone who spent a great deal of time out of doors. He was dressed in typical home-spun clothing, his jacket and boots made of tanned hide.

"Praise the Powers," he said, smiling widely. "You have no idea how glad I was to spot your fire. I've been lost in this thrice be damned forest for two days now." He eased the pack he was wearing to the ground and held his hands out to the fire's warmth.

"Who are you?" Rayne asked timidly.

"Gervais is the name, good lady."

"What are you doing out here?" Pyre asked, a little less friendly. It seemed too much of a co-incident after everything that happened at the village to run into a complete stranger out here. For all they knew he could be one of the raiders, sent back to make sure there were no survivors.

Rayne laid a hand on his arm. She could feel the heat, even through his heavy jacket. Quick as a thought, the air around them grew cooler. "Why don't we sit down and Gervais can tell us his story?"

For a moment she thought he was going to argue, but then he nodded sharply. His foster mother had drilled courtesy into him and it would be very discourteous to turn away a fellow traveler from their fire. If the man was indeed a raider, they'd figure it out soon enough.

When they were all seated around the fire, Gervais continued with his story. "I've been to Alderwood to visit my brother and do a little trading. I'm a farmer by profession, but I do a little wood carving to trade. I get a better price for my goods in the city, but my brother's been feeling poorly and I wanted to make sure he was all right."

"That's very commendable," Rayne told him.

Gervais looked a little embarrassed. "Yes, well." He coughed. "I was just starting back and the weather went crazy – I've never seen so much snow this time of year."

Rayne and Pyre exchanged a look as Gervais shook his head.

"When it melted, the run-off caused a flash flood, just as I was crossing at the Way Station. Swept me and my horse downstream. Lost my horse and I've spent the last two days looking for the road again." He coughed again.

"Are you all right?" Rayne asked.

Gervais waved away her concern. "I'm fine, just a little congested from my dip in the river. It's pretty cold for swimming, this time of year. Where are you folks headed? I heard there was a little village tucked away around here somewhere, you from there?"

"We haven't seen a village," Pyre said. "My wife and I are from Mountainview, several days to the north. We're headed to the city to seek work."

Ducking her head, Rayne tried not to smile at Pyre's smooth lies. The Mother's instructions had included the advice that they have a story ready, just in case they ran into someone with questions. Apparently Pyre had thought of one.

"Ah, you young folks. Can't stay away from the technology, can you? My neighbor's lad went off to the city, last we heard he got a job at the spaceport. Guess the quiet life just can't compare."

Pyre shrugged. "There was little work to be had in Mountainview."

"Is your farm to the north or the south on the road?" Rayne asked. "Perhaps you would like to travel with us."

"Why that's very kind of you. The farm should only be a day or two away, once we reach the road. I insist that you and your husband spend the night with us. You can't beat my wife's cooking and she loves having company."

Pyre tuned out the rest of their conversation. What had possessed him to claim Rayne as his wife? The idea seemed to pop into his head and out of his mouth before he was even aware of it. He'd fully intended to present them as brother and sister, this was just going to make everything that much harder.

Gervais seemed harmless enough, but Pyre couldn't seem to relax. Just having the man sharing their fire set his teeth on edge. How much worse was it going to be when they were surrounded by a whole city of people?

What if they got separated or one of them became injured? What if one of them lost control of their element?

Chapter Ten

From Wynne's Journal:

Plans are being made by the humans for a sanctuary for both the humans and the Elementals involved in our movement. I do not know what form it will take, nor where it is to be located, but my contact assures me it will provide the safety we all crave. Dr. Arjun has been closeted in his lab with his two most trusted assistants. The rest of us wait in fear. Another technician has disappeared and again we do not know why. By twos and threes the humans with Elemental foster-children have begun to vanish from the town but Dr. Arjun does not notice because there are always other families to take their place. I do not know how they have arranged this, nor do I really care. The newcomers are naturally curious about the compound and are not easily discouraged. I fear they may cause trouble before we are finished here – timing will be everything.

Before long, Rayne's side of the conversation was being punctuated by yawns.

"Forgive me, good sir, kind lady. Here I am taking advantage of your kindness and keeping you from your rest. I didn't mean to run on so. My wife says I could talk the birds down from the trees."

"Do not let it worry you," Rayne told him. "My husband, as you have seen, is not much for conversation. Your company is most welcome."

She sent a teasing look Pyre's way and it was all he could do not to roll his eyes in return. He hadn't missed the way she seemed to linger over the word husband either.

"I thank you most kindly. Might I ask the names of my benefactors?"

"Oh!" Rayne gave a start. "You must forgive our rudeness. We are not used to any company other than our own."

"I am Pryne," Pyre said quickly, shooting Rayne a look. "My wife is Raya."

Rayne had her mouth open to answer Gervais and quickly shut it. She was careful not to let her surprise show on her face. False names? Was that really necessary? Apparently to Pyre it was.

"There's a chill in the air tonight," she said instead. "We have plenty of blankets if you are in need."

Though his bedroll had survived his dunking in the river, Gervais accepted the loan of one of their thermal blankets gratefully. He made himself comfortable on the opposite side of the fire and within seconds was snoring gently.

Pyre lay down beside Rayne, putting her between himself and the fire. There were too many thoughts and misgivings swirling around in his head. Something nagged at his mind, a little thing but it was important. Something to do with Rayne's hand resting on his arm when Gervais first approached their fire . . . The harder he chased the thought, the further it slipped away until at last he fell into a troubled sleep.

Though he had laid their bedrolls out side by side, in the morning he was not surprised to awaken with Rayne in his arms. It was getting to be a habit and if he was honest with himself it was a habit he could learn to enjoy. How unfortunate that it wasn't going to last.

By the time the others stirred, he'd already stoked the fire and started something hot for their breakfast. Though his cough seemed to have disappeared, Gervais looked slightly flushed in the morning light.

"Are you sure you're all right?" Rayne asked him. She had some experience treating illness, that was why she'd been one of the few chosen to attend the Mother, but neither she nor Pyre could afford to become sick.

Gervais waved away her concern. "It's nothing, really. Once I'm home I'll rest up a bit and be good as new."

Filled with misgivings, Rayne let the subject go.

They were closer to the road than they expected and reached it by mid-day. As roads went it wasn't much to look at, a wide dirt track that curved gently to the north in one direction and a sharper curve to the south in the other. The trees were considerably thinner here; they were almost out of the forest. Gervais looked around for landmarks, brightening up considerably when he realized where they were.

"The farm's just a few hours away," he said excitedly. "I can't wait! A hot bath, a soft bed – spending the night out in the woods is for you young people, not the likes of me."

"You must be looking forward to seeing your wife," Rayne said, slanting a look sideways at Pyre. He snorted under his breath and started leading the way forward.

"Ah, yes. Let me tell you about my wife, Maisie. The best woman a man could ever hope for. Did I tell you what an excellent cook she was? Even better than your man Pryne here . . ."

Pyre let the droning voice fade into the background. He no longer believed Gervais to be associated with the raiders. The way the man ran off at the mouth he'd be more of a liability than an asset to any raid. Even Rayne wasn't able to get more than a word or two into the conversation going on behind him.

It was a shame, really. He liked listening to her voice. Rayne had a cool, soothing cadence to her voice, like a mountain stream flowing over the moss covered rocks. Even her silence was restful, like a draught from a forest spring.

What was the matter with him? Since when had he waxed poetic about anything, let alone a woman? He should be avoiding thinking of her, not dwelling on the sound of her voice, the feel of her in his arms, the softness of her skin . . . then there was also the promise he made to the Mother.

Ruthlessly breaking off that train of thought he stumbled, and she was right there at his elbow. "Are you all right?" she asked.

He flushed in the face of her concern. "I'm fine," he told her, feeling anything but that.

* * * * *

They reached Gervais's farm just as the sun began lowering in the sky. It was a typical looking set-up. A path led to the house – more of a compact, two-story cabin. There was a garden on one side of it with a few vines still bearing autumn vegetables. A little ways away from the house, on the other side, was a barn. Beside the barn was a small pen with a few pigs and a larger enclosure holding a pair of horses. Chickens roamed freely between the house and the barn.

They were only halfway up the path, Gervais leading the way, when the door to the farmhouse flew open. A short, stout woman stood framed in the doorway, fists resting on her ample hips.

"Gervais, you good for nothing, worthless man! Where have you been? You were only supposed to be gone for two days and it's been almost a week! The horse came back yesterday!"

"Ah, Maisie my love," he hurried to greet her, enveloping her in a hug. "Such an adventure I've had! And I'd be adventuring still if it wasn't for the fortune of meeting new friends." He turned her so she could see Rayne and Pyre where they'd stopped a few feet away.

Maisie wriggled free of his embrace. "Let go of me, you great oaf, and introduce me!"

"This is Pryne and Raya, on their way to the city to seek their fortunes. And this, my young friends," he continued, resting his hands on the shoulders of his wife, "is my darling Maisie."

"I feel I know you already," Rayne said with a smile.

Maisie waved a dismissive hand in the air. "Don't believe half of what Gervais says, he always runs off at the mouth. Welcome to our home. Please, come inside. You must be weary."

Before Rayne and Pyre knew what was happening, she'd drawn them into the house and shown them around, leaving them in a bedroom to freshen up while she went to see if there was anything to eat.

Rayne looked curiously around the room they'd been given. It was similar to her room in the village, the village that was no longer there. She sat down heavily on the bed.

"What's wrong?" Pyre asked, turning from the window he'd been looking out of.

She shook her head. "It's nothing. I'm just a little tired."

Although she did look tired, he knew it was more than that. Unfortunately, he didn't know what he could do about it. He wasn't good with people, he never had been. While he was still searching for something comforting to say, she got up with a ghost of a smile on her face.

"We'd better not keep our hosts waiting."

Pyre sighed and followed her down the stairs. Maisie was just setting several steaming bowls on the table. Gervais stood at one end carving a roast.

"I can't believe you prepared this so quickly!" Rayne exclaimed.

"It was actually already made, I just had to warm it up," Maisie confessed. "Sit! Eat!"

They did as they were told. Gervais had been right when he described her as a force of nature. She was also as good a cook as he'd promised and Pyre unbent enough to tell her so.

"Why thank you young man," she said, beaming. "I—" The rest of what she said was lost as Gervais began coughing. She laid the back of her hand against his forehead and clucked in concern. "Why didn't you tell me you weren't feeling well?"

"I'm fine. Just picked up a bit of a cold from that dunking in the river. No need to worry."

"I'm your wife. It's my job to worry. Now get on up to bed."

Grumbling, he did as he was told. Rayne helped Maisie clear the table and then gently shooed her out of the kitchen.

"We can do the rest. Why don't you take a cup of tea up to Gervais?" She could tell that Maisie was more worried than she let on.

Maisie was happy to do as she suggested. Pyre and Rayne finished doing the dishes and cleaning up the kitchen, then went up to their room as well.

"Which side do you want?" Rayne asked, indicating the bed.

"Rayne, I don't think we should—" He didn't think it mattered which side of the bed he slept on, sleeping together was not a good idea. Something of what he was thinking must have shown on his face.

"You don't need to worry," she snapped. "I promise I won't throw myself at you." She turned her back to him and started pulling off her clothing, keeping only enough on for modesty's sake. Choosing the side closest to her, she climbed into bed and shut her eyes.

She was tired and angry, not at Pyre, but at herself. If she could just confide her secret to him he'd

see why there wasn't a problem with them being together. But she just couldn't. Not yet, anyway.

Chapter Eleven

From Wynne's Journal:
The compound is in an uproar. One of the subjects from Dr. Arjun's breeding program is missing. Dr. Arjun is beside himself. He has interrogated each of us in turn but everyone has been able to account for their whereabouts. Security has been increased in the compound and he has even sent several of his most trusted followers to the village to see if someone from there might have seen something, but she seems to have vanished without a trace. Dr. Arjun fears she may find her way to the city where she can contact the Ardraci or even the Ilezie. He is making plans to move the entire compound to a more secure location. It will take time to make all the arrangements, and when the time comes, we will be ready to make our break. Meanwhile, we are trapped inside the compound with all the others.

The pleasure of sleeping in a proper bed was diminished by the fact they started out the night with their backs to each other, lying stiff and uncomfortable. Rayne was already up and dressed before Pyre awoke in the morning. He wondered if they shifted during the night, ending up cuddled together, and he wondered what she thought of it if they had.

Pyre was slow getting ready. He'd had too little sleep since first rescuing Rayne on the mountain and it was catching up with him. There was nothing he'd like more than to just fall back into bed, but they had to keep moving. He wasn't sure how far it was to the city but they needed to reach it as quickly as possible.

When he finally made his way downstairs, Rayne was just finishing her breakfast. They needed to talk, to clear the air between them, but there was nothing they could say in front of Maisie.

"I was just telling Raya that Gervaise is feeling a little under the weather from his adventure and I have him resting today. He wanted to have me try and persuade you to stay longer, but your wife has explained that her sister is awaiting you in the city."

"Uh, yes. That's right." Pyre was having a hard time organizing his thoughts. "We wouldn't want to disappoint her, or worry her." He coughed faintly.

Ignoring the look Rayne gave him, he concentrated on the plate Maisie slid in front of him. Though the breakfast was hot and delicious, he found he had little appetite. He forced himself to eat it anyway, knowing he'd need the energy for the day ahead.

When he finished, Maisie had a basket prepared for them. "Just a little something for the road," she said.

"You shouldn't have, really," Rayne told her.

"Pish! It's nothing compared to you bringing my Gervais home to me. You'll make good time now that you've reached the road. There's an inn just outside the city, with any luck you should make it that far by tomorrow."

They thanked her again for her hospitality, then shouldered their packs and followed the path to the road. Turning, they waved at Maisie standing in the doorway, then continued on their way.

"They seemed like a nice, normal couple," Rayne said after a while, breaking the silence between them.

"Yes, they did."

"I wonder if they ever had any children, they never mentioned any."

"I don't know."

"Do you think people will be like that in the city?"

"I don't know."

"Maisie didn't say anything, but I think she's worried about Gervais. Do you think he'll be all right?"

"Probably."

"Are *you* feeling all right?"

"I'm fine," he said, a little more sharply than he intended. "I just don't feel like talking."

"Oh."

Just one little word, but it seemed to hold a world of hurt in it. Pyre didn't know what the matter was with him. Rayne was trying to mend the rift between them and he just couldn't muster the energy to do his part. She deserved better than that.

"I'm sorry," he said with a sigh. "I'm guess I'm still pretty tired. I'll be glad when we reach the city and can have a proper rest."

"It's all right," she said quietly. "I know I tend to talk too much. My mother always said I talk just to hear the sound of my own voice."

"I like the sound of your voice," he said.

Rayne glanced at him in surprise but he didn't seem to be aware of having said anything. Maybe there was hope for the two of them yet.

Pyre set an easy pace for them, for which Rayne was grateful. She thought of what the Mother had told her about Pyre, and of his confession just before Gervais found them, saving her from confessing her secret in return.

She adjusted the strap of her pack where it was digging into her shoulder and then lengthened her stride to catch up to Pyre who didn't seem to realize she'd fallen behind.

Although her secret would make him see there was no reason they couldn't be together, it was also the very thing that would turn him from her. The more time she spent with him the more he meant to her – she wasn't ready to lose him.

The least she could do, however, was let him know that his confession didn't change anything between them.

"Pyre," she said hesitantly. "About the other night . . ."

"What night?"

"The night Gervais found us, about what you told me. I—"

There was a hitch in his step but he recovered quickly. "We should focus on our task," he said. "I don't know what came over me that night, but it's not something I'm prepared to discuss, at least not right now."

"But—"

He glanced at her, then back at the road ahead. "I know it changes things, but we need to get to the city and get that message sent. If you still feel the need to talk . . . we can talk after the message is sent."

Rayne ground her teeth in frustration. "All right," she agreed grudgingly. "I'll let it go for now, but we will talk about this, sooner or later."

They spent the night in a way station, one of the shelters built for travelers that were spaced several miles apart along the road. It was little more than a shack, but it was clean and dry and had a stone fireplace.

Rayne had been surprised, but not unduly worried when Pyre fell asleep before she finished making their evening meal. He had mentioned needing rest; their forced journey was obviously starting to catch up with him. But she was awake before he was as well and that sent a frisson of alarm through her.

Pyre felt irritable and out of sorts. He hadn't slept well. The way station was too warm and the ground was too hard. He was getting tired of sleeping on the ground. Rayne hovered around him like a pest and it was all he could do not to snap at her.

He pulled out the map the Mother had included with her instructions and looked at it carefully. "With any luck we should make the city before nightfall."

"Good," Rayne said. "After spending the night in a real bed, it was not easy sleeping on the ground again."

He grunted a response and folded the map back up, tucking it into his pack. Rayne resigned herself to another long day of silence.

It was a beautiful day. The sun shone down, its light filtered through the leaves overhead. A wisp of a breeze rustled the leaves of the trees, bringing the sweet smell of late autumn flowers. Birdsong filled the air.

Pyre began to cough just after they stopped for their mid-day meal. He tried to cover it by pretending he'd choked on his food, but Rayne wasn't fooled. He seemed distracted, lethargic, and there was a faint flush to his skin.

She was about to suggest they stop at the next way station but realized it would be best to keep moving. If Pyre was getting sick, they could find help in the city. She didn't ask him if he was feeling all right, he would have just lied to her anyway, but she kept an eye on him the rest of the afternoon.

The sun had just begun lowering in the sky when they reached the edge of the city. At first it was much like the village, a few outlying farms and then the odd house, but the further they went the more closely the houses were built.

They'd encountered the odd traveler on the road, going in the opposite direction, but as they neared the city they encountered more and more people, some on foot and some in wagons or riding saddle beasts. Some of these people nodded in acknowledgment, a few smiled and call out a pleasant greeting, and some just ignored them.

The road became a hard packed surface and more roads intersected it. Twice they had to move aside to allow passage for a large, heavily burdened wagon. A few shops appeared and then, to Rayne's great relief, they found an inn.

Rayne took charge and got them a room, ordering a meal to be sent up. Pyre followed her up the stairs, hardly knowing what he was doing. He sat on the bed and watched listlessly as she stowed their gear. The smell of their dinner, when it arrived, nauseated him and he lay down on the bed.

"Pyre," Rayne said, sitting down beside him. "You have to try and eat something."

"Not now," he said, eyes closed. "I'll eat later."

"You need to eat now," she said sharply. "You're sick. You've been fighting it for the last two days."

"I'm just tired, that's all. I just need some rest. I'll be fine after some rest."

"You're not fine! You have a fever, it—"

At the word fever his eyes snapped open and he struggled to sit up. "Help me up, I have to get out of here! Damn it, I should have known what was happening to me."

"Pyre, where do you think you're going?" Rayne fought to keep him in the bed.

"I'm a Fire Elemental, a fever is deadly. It can make me lose control of my element. Why do you think I lived in a cave instead of a cabin?"

"It's all right, Pyre. Nothing will happen, I promise you."

"The whole city could burn," he said, the fight going out of him. "I can't have any more deaths on my conscience."

"No one is going to die," she soothed. "You have to trust me. I can control your fire."

Chapter Twelve

From Wynne's Journal:
It's good that we already had a plan in place. Dr. Arjun has found a new location for the compound. All we know is that it's away from any human settlements. He's doubled the security here and his most trusted assistants are over-seeing the packing. The tension is beginning to wear on us all. Our little group is twelve strong and we each have our assignments that have nothing to do with helping move the compound. By this time tomorrow we will either have made our escape or we will be dead in the attempt. So much depends on our success! It is not just of ourselves we must think, but of the children we have already saved as well. Though the humans who have the care of them know the children are gifted, they do not truly know what it means to be an Elemental. Even we do not know what will happen when their powers begin to manifest.

Pyre woke slowly. What he could see of the room he was in was unfamiliar, as was the feel of the bed beneath him. His throat was dry and he had a mild headache, but otherwise he felt fine. Frowning, he tried to remember where he was, and what had happened to him.

He'd been sick, running a fever. His eyes widened suddenly. Pain spiked through his head as he sat up too quickly. He looked all around him, including upwards at the heavy beamed ceiling, but there was no trace of burn marks. When he inhaled deeply he could detect no hint of smoke.

He lay back down and tried to gather his scattered thoughts. He remembered starting to feel ill on the road and arriving at the inn. He remembered Rayne telling him he had a fever and struggling with her as he tried to leave. The rest was just a blur, except . . . she had said something to him. Something significant. If only he could remember!

There was a noise at the door and Rayne entered, carrying a tray. A smile lit her face as she realized he was awake.

"I was beginning to think you'd never awaken," she said. The teasing note in her voice did nothing to disguise the worry in her eyes. "How are you feeling?"

Pyre struggled to sit up again and she set the tray down to help him.

"I—" he coughed, his dry throat closing up on him.

Rayne handed him a mug with something cool in it and he sipped gratefully. An involuntary grimace passed over his face at the taste. That brought a genuine smile to her face.

"It tastes bad, I know, but it will speed your recovery."

He looked at the mug in resignation. Better to get it over with than to prolong the process. Tipping it up he drank the rest of the contents all at once.

With a shudder, he handed the empty mug back to Rayne. "How long was I ill?"

"Including the length of time you were ill on the road, or just how long you've been ill since we reached the inn? No, don't bother," she said, holding up a hand when he opened his mouth. "Did you really think you were helping by trying to hide the fact you were ill?"

Pyre looked closer at her. She was pale, much paler than usual, and there were dark circles under her eyes. When was the last time she slept?

"We've been here three nights," she told him. "Your fever broke early this morning. This virus spread quickly; there were already several fallen ill with it before we got here. It's the only reason we were allowed to stay."

"Why weren't you infected?" he asked, a little peevishly.

Another genuine, but faint smile. "I appear to be one of the few immune to the disease. Now here," she placed the tray on his lap. "You need to build your strength."

The tray held a bowl of thick soup that smelled as heavenly as it looked. There was freshly baked bread to go with it, as well as a soft yellow cheese that could be spread on the bread. Pyre was suddenly ravenous.

He was silent while he ate, but watched Rayne as she wandered around the room, flicking a curtain back into place, arranging a chair just slightly to the side. The question kept repeating in his mind. If he'd had a fever for three days, how had she kept him from losing control of his element?

When he was finished he set the tray aside, suddenly aware of a more pressing need.

"Rayne, I need—" he squirmed slightly as she turned to look at him. "What I mean is, is there someplace . . ."

Understanding lit her face. "The sanitary facilities are through that door there," she said, pointing to the door on the opposite side of the room. She watched him struggle to get out of bed. "Do you need any help?"

"No!" he said in a panic when she took a step towards him. "I'm sure I can manage on my own."

Pyre was appalled by how shaky he was on his feet. Stubbornly, he clung to the need to stay upright and made his way unsteadily to the door. Once it was shut behind him he breathed a sigh of relief.

Three days, three days they had lost because of him! If the Ilezie were not able to pick up the trail of the raiders and the children were lost, it would be his fault. And how long would this damnable weakness last? More time lost!

The thought came to him that he could send Rayne on ahead with the message, but just as quickly he dismissed it as a bad idea. This was no quiet village they were in, this was the city. A woman alone would be prey to all kinds of danger, especially a woman as beautiful as Rayne.

How had she managed to keep his fire at bay? He didn't for one moment believe he'd been able to stay in control of his element the whole time he had a fever burning inside him. The time for their talk was long overdue.

He left the sanitary facilities intent on confronting Rayne, only to find her curled up on the bed, fast asleep. She looked so peaceful, the lines of stress and worry gone from her face, that he didn't have the heart to wake her.

Lying down beside her, he brushed a stray strand of hair from her face. She murmured in her sleep, turning into his touch. Pyre sighed, and resigned himself to waiting a little longer for his answers.

* * * * *

When Rayne awoke it was to find Pyre lying propped up on one elbow beside her, watching her.

"I remember clearly the last time I had a fever," he told her. "It was just after I went through my *tespiro*. I set my bed on fire three times before they moved me to the cave near the Mother. She was the only one who could stay with me, of course I didn't know at the time it was because she was a Fire Elemental."

Eyes wide in a suddenly pale face, Rayne moved to get up. Pyre's hand shot out to grip her wrist, keeping her in place.

He continued, in a conversational tone. "One of the things Mother forever worried over was my lack of control. Though I'm able to cope with day to day situations, I still have trouble when it comes to stress . . . or illness. So how is it I was ill with a fever for three nights and there is no sign of my element escaping?"

"I—I don't know," she stammered. "P—Perhaps you have more control that you realize."

"I think perhaps I am not the only one with a secret to tell," he said softly. "You said you can control my fire. Did you say that to keep me from leaving or can you really do what you said you can."

She jerked her wrist free and rolled over to sit on the edge of the bed, head hanging in defeat.

"I wanted to tell you, I tried to tell you, but I just couldn't," she said in a small voice.

Pyre moved so that he was sitting beside her. "I trusted you with my darkest secret," he said gently. "Can you not trust me in return?"

"It's not a matter of trust . . . it's—" She couldn't bring herself to face him. "My gift is . . . different. Not really a true gift at all."

He put his hand over hers for encouragement. Her fingers twined with his but she still wouldn't look at him.

Rayne took a deep breath. "I have the ability to draw on the energy of other elements."

"I don't understand."

"It started just after I passed the age for *tespiro*. At first I did it subconsciously, not even realizing what I was doing. But others soon began to find being around me . . . draining. Mother figured out what was happening. She worked with me day and night until I could control it."

"You can draw on elemental energy? But that's not . . ." his voice trailed off as he considered all the ramifications.

"Possible? I wouldn't have believed it either, if it hadn't happened to me. Mother tried to keep it quiet, but there was one time . . . afterwards most of the others just shunned me."

Pyre put his arm around her. "Your gift is terrible in its power, but at least you have control of it. I don't understand why anyone would shun you for it."

"There's more." Rayne hunched in further on herself. "The energy I take needs to be released but before I can do this I . . . change it."

"Change it? Change it how?"

"I—I twist it into a new form, one related to water."

"So you were able to siphon off the excess fire from my fever and turn it into . . . what?"

"I have little control over what form the energy takes. At first there was so much it became a terrible storm, then it diminished into a vast fog bank."

Her head hung in shame. She couldn't bring herself to look at him. Voices from the past filled her mind, the ones calling her unnatural and abomination. Now that Pyre knew her secret, he would turn from her in disgust, as the others had. "I understand if you wish to travel no further with me."

"Why wouldn't I?" he asked, his surprise genuine.

"Because I am not natural, I am an abomination."

Pyre took her by the shoulders and turned her so she was facing him. "You are not an abomination, any more than I am."

Shocked, her gaze flew upwards to meet his. "But —"

"You have a gift, we both do. Yours is unique and should be a source of pride, not shame."

"Pride? But I—"

"If it hadn't been for you I would have burned down this inn, possibly starting a fire that would consume the whole city."

"You aren't disgusted by me?" she couldn't help asking.

"Far from it. In fact, now that I know your secret I'm finally free to do what I've wanted for days."

"What's that?" she asked, suddenly breathless from the banked fire in his eyes.

"This," he told her, head lowering towards hers.

Chapter Thirteen

From Wynne's Journal:

There were twelve us in the beginning. Three sacrificed themselves to give the rest of us the opportunity to escape. Three more died as we fled the compound. We brought with us what children we were able, and passed these on to the waiting humans, then went our separate ways to avoid discovery. When we reached the first rendezvous point we came to the painful decision that we could not do this ourselves. We must contact the home world and send for the Ilezie. While I and the others wait at the village closest to the next meeting place, Kadhri and Aden have travelled onwards to the space port. There's said to be a temple dedicated to Nishon there, from which we can send our message. Fear preys on me as we wait. I was against separating our group, it's too soon. What if something goes wrong? What if the home world does not believe us? What if Dr. Arjun discovers us before we can send for help? What if, what if.

Zavion says I worry needlessly but I cannot shake this feeling of impending doom.

His kiss was gentle, perfect really. So perfect in fact that it brought tears to her eyes. He pulled away immediately.

"Rayne? Are you all right? I'm sorry if I—"

"No, it's not you. I just . . ." she ducked her head down in embarrassment. "I cannot believe you are not turning from me."

"Why would I do that?" he asked, genuinely puzzled.

"I am unclean," she whispered. "Nothing more than a parasite."

"A parasite? Why would you think such a thing?"

She shook her head mutely unable to meet his eyes.

"Rayne, talk to me," he said gently.

Shoulders slumped, eyes on the floor, Rayne began to speak. "I had few friends growing up, even before my *tespiro*. The other children were uncomfortable around me, but no one knew why."

"It must have been very lonely for you."

"It wasn't so bad, and I did have one close friend. Her name was Dhara." There was a hitch in her voice. He waited patiently for her to go on. "She was an Earth Elemental. We used to joke that when we both came into our powers we'd make mud together." She smiled in remembrance, but it quickly faded.

"I had already undergone my *tespiro* and the Mother was working with me on my control . . ." Rayne shifted uncomfortably. She would rather be anywhere than here, having this conversation, but if there was to be anything between her and Pyre he deserved to know the whole truth.

"Dhara's *tespiro* was . . . she was earth, remember, and our village depended greatly on the earth for our sustenance. Somehow she was poisoning the land around her and nothing the Mother tried could stop it. The Mother asked me . . . it was all done in secrecy. I was able to draw off Dhara's power - it was the first time I ever consciously used my gift."

There had to be more to it than that. Pyre waited patiently for her to continue.

"Afterwards, the Mother swore her to secrecy, but it was Dhara who . . . she . . ." Rayne fell silent.

"Let me guess," Pyre said grimly. "It was Dhara who called you an abomination and a parasite, and it was Dhara who turned the others against you."

Rayne nodded. "Dhara blamed me for the fact her gift was so small in comparison to others."

"The energy you drew from Dhara, what form did it take?"

"What?" Rayne's head came up and she looked at him in surprise. Whatever else she had been expecting, it had not been this.

"When you released her energy," he said patiently. "What happened?"

"There was a cleansing rain. It only lasted a few hours, but it seemed to help set the land to rights again."

"No floods, no torrential rains?"

"No," she replied, thoroughly puzzled.

"Think about it Rayne," he urged. "When you drew the energy off of me what happened?"

"You know what happened! I—oh!" She finally figured out what he was driving at. "If Dhara's powers had been stronger, so would the rain storm that was created." She looked at him, almost not daring to believe. "It was nothing I had done, her gift was not large to begin with."

Pyre put his arms around her and pulled her close. "You are no more to blame for Dhara than I am for Angana." As he said this, he felt something within him lighten. It was the first time in years he'd felt at peace with himself.

This time, Rayne didn't try to stop the tears that came. Like the rain from Dhara's energy, it was a cleansing. Pyre held her, stroking her hair, her back, whispering soothing nonsense. They took comfort in each other as the ghosts of the past were finally laid to rest. Her tears slowed then finally stopped.

"All those years," she said, head resting on his shoulder. "I blamed myself for Dhara's lack of power."

"And I blamed myself for the death of Angana."

"And yet," she said slowly, "I would change nothing of the past, for it led me to you."

Pyre turned so that he was facing her again. She looked up at him hesitantly at first, gauging his reaction. Whatever she saw must have been reassuring, for she met the fire igniting in him with one of her own.

He dipped his head slowly, allowing her time to pull away if this wasn't what she wanted. Her heart stuttered in her chest as his lips touched hers and a shiver ran through her. He pulled back slightly.

"Are you sure about this?" he asked, eyes searching hers.

She reached up and touched his cheek with her fingertips. "I'm very sure about this."

He took her hand in his and turned it over so he could kiss her palm. Rayne shuddered as the sensation shot right through her. Using her hand to pull her towards him, he wrapped his arms around her and kissed her again. He was gentle at first, becoming more demanding as she began to respond.

Her hands went to his hair, sinking into the silky softness as she pressed closer. A throbbing filled her. Her breasts tingled and she was filled with a molten heat that had nothing to do with the heat he was generating. When he slipped one of his hands between them to cup her breast through her soft shirt she cried out, arching into his touch. She needed more, much more.

Loosening his hold, he slipped from her grasp and knelt in front of her. Slowly he began to undress her, worshiping her with his hands and his lips as he peeled away the layers of clothing. Her breath was coming in pants by the time he was finished, her skin flushed to a rosy hue. She watched with heavy-lidded eyes as he divested himself of his own clothing. Gently he moved her so she was lying on the bed and then lay down beside her.

"You're so beautiful," he whispered, unable to take his eyes off her. "I could be happy just lying here looking at you forever."

"Well I could not," Rayne said, rolling onto her side, facing him. He, too, was beautiful, at least in her eyes.

Pushing him onto his back she ran one hand over the sculpted planes of his chest, reveling in the con- trast between the soft skin and the hard muscles un- derneath. She scraped her nails over one flat, male nipple and he hissed an intake of breath. Flames licked across his skin. Without conscious thought she began to siphon the heat from him. It began to rain outside, the drops beating against the closed shutters.

Her fingers traced over a series of four parallel scars on his left pectoral. "What happened here?"

"Got too close to a bear," he rasped.

Rayne's eyes widened. "Really?" Without waiting for an answer she leaned over and kissed his scar. He groaned as she used the tip of her tongue to trace each of the four furrows.

"What about this one?" She moved lower to a jagged line on his abdomen.

"Rock fall," he gasped.

Again she traced it with her tongue, enjoying the way his skin shivered under her touch.

The rain outside was coming down heavier, the noise as it pelted the shutters increasing. A rumble of thunder could be heard in the distance.

"Enough!" he pleaded as she prepared to move lower. Before she realized what was happening he reached out, flipped her onto her back, and was looming over her. "My turn," he told her.

Propping himself up on one elbow, he used the opposite hand to trace a fine, blue vein that showed through the pale skin of her neck and upper chest. He'd never felt anything as soft as her skin.

Her already hard nipples puckered even tighter in anticipation. He stroked down the center of her torso then rested his hand flat on her stomach, bypassing her breasts.

"You're skin is incredibly soft."

She wriggled under his touch as his hand traced up her side and across, then down the other side – everywhere but where she most wanted to be touched. His knuckles scraped the underside of her breasts then moved back down to her stomach. Unable to stand it any longer she reached for him, but he stayed just out of her reach.

The wind began to pick up as the rain lashed down. Thunder cracked and lightning hit the tower of a building in the next block.

"Pyre, please!"

"Well, since you're begging so sweetly . . ."

He leaned over and kissed her, one hand going to her breast and squeezing gently, thumb flicking over her nipple. She moaned at the exquisite torture then cried out as his mouth replaced his hand. Back and forth he went between her breasts until she was quivering with tension.

"I can't wait any longer," she gasped. "Please," she begged, not even sure at this point what she was begging for.

Giving each rosy-tipped breast one last kiss, Pyre nudged her legs apart and moved over her. He sank slowly into her soft, wet, heat then stopped, allowing her body time to adjust. They were a perfect fit, as he'd known they would be. Rayne moved restlessly beneath him.

He kissed her as he started to stroke in and out. She rose to meet each thrust, wrapping her legs around his hips for better purchase. Rayne didn't know if it was something to do with the sharing of their element or if it was just because this had been so long in coming, but she couldn't seem to get close enough to him.

Pyre caught some of her frantic need and sped up, driving into her over and over. Her breath was coming in small gasps and she was covered in a fine sheen of sweat. They reached completion at the same time, crying out with one voice. Afterward Pyre rolled to one side, taking her with him. The storm outside raged on as they slept, oblivious.

Chapter Fourteen

From Wynne's Journal:

I am alone now. Kadhri and Aden are dead. Their bodies were found alongside the road to the city. It is believed they were the victims of bandits, but Zavion and I believed it was the work of Dr. Arjun. I feared he would have the ways into the city watched, and it appears I was correct. Zavion called my ability to sense these things uncanny. I call it useless if no one will heed my warnings. We agreed that we could not risk another attempt to contact the home world — to fail would mean leaving both the children and their foster parents without guidance. Then Fadri and Vahi disappeared. We do not know whether they went off on their own or were taken. Before Zavion and I could continue on our own there was a fire in the inn where we had our rooms. My gift, such as it is, is fire, and small though it is it was enough to allow me to escape. Zavion was of the earth, and perished. Now I, alone, must see that the children are raised properly. I only hope I am up to the task.

Pyre was the first to awaken in the morning, Rayne still nestled in his arms. He had never contemplated his sole existence before but now he realized it would be difficult going back to being alone when this was over. Rayne had pushed her way into his life and burrowed her way into his heart. He may not know what the future held for them, but he knew it would be bleak indeed without her at his side.

She stirred and sighed, snuggling closer. Pyre smiled and kissed the top of her head. "I would like nothing more than to stay like this," he told her. "But we must get the message sent to the Ilezie."

Rayne stirred again, then came fully awake. Pushing herself upright she looked down at him, a flicker of guilt in her eyes.

"No," he admonished, pulling her down for a quick kiss. "There's no need to feel guilty. We could not have sent the message last night, and there is no shame in what we shared."

She allowed herself to relax against him once more, sliding one hand over his chest. "Of all the things I feel over making love with you, shame is not one of them."

"What do you feel?" he couldn't help asking.

"Wonderful." She lifted her head slightly to smile at him. "Complete. And if it were not for our mission I would find a way to keep you here and repeat last night over and over again."

He couldn't have stopped the grin of pure, male, satisfaction that slid over his face if he'd wanted to. "If we're lucky, maybe there will be a lengthy wait until these Ilezie arrive to help."

Stretching upwards, she kissed him, but wriggled away when he tried to bring his arms around her again. "We must go send the message," she admonished, voice tinged with regret.

Pyre sighed, "You're right, of course. But you'd better dress quickly or I may not be able to restrain myself."

Still smiling, she slipped from the bed, picking up her scattered clothing as she crossed to the bathing chamber. He waited until the door closed behind her before getting up to search for his own clothing. When she returned he was fully dressed, sitting on the edge of the bed combing out his hair.

"Would you like me to do that for you?" she asked, almost shyly.

He nodded and wordlessly held out the comb. She climbed on the bed behind him and gently began running the comb through his hair. The intimacy of it made his gut clench. When she finished untangling it, she swiftly braided it, tying off the end with the leather cord he had lying on the bed beside him.

"There, all done," she said, voice husky.

"We should go before I drag you back into this bed," he said.

There was a hitch in her breathing. "Yes."

He didn't know if she was agreeing they should go, or agreeing to be dragged back into bed, and he didn't much care. Turning, he put his arms around her and dragged her across his lap, smothering her gasp of surprise with a searing kiss.

Pyre felt his skin heating up, and just as quickly the heat disappeared. The sound of rain pattering on the roof could be heard.

"Damn." He broke off the kiss and rested his forehead against hers, breathing heavily. "I'm sorry, I —"

"Don't be," she said, her own breathing not quite steady. "I'm certainly not."

They sat like that a few moments longer before he reluctantly loosened his hold on her. "We should get moving," he said regretfully.

There were still plenty of the Mother's credits left and they treated themselves to breakfast in the tap room below.

"It's nice to see you up and around," the innkeeper said to Pyre. "That wife of yours is a devoted little thing, barely left your side to eat."

"Yes, I'm a lucky man," Pyre said, with a smile.

" 'Course with the storms we've been having most people with any sense have been staying indoors."

"Storms you say?" He looked across the table at Rayne who refused to meet his eyes but blushed prettily.

The innkeeper nodded. "Terrible storms. Never seen the like before. This isn't the season for them either. You two take care if you're going out today." With that he bustled away to greet a new customer.

The rain from earlier had dissipated and the sun was starting to shine as Pyre and Rayne left the inn.

"Did the Mother say how we are to send the message to the Ilezie?" Rayne asked.

"We need to go to the temple of Nishon," Pyre said absently, studying the city map he'd asked the innkeeper for.

"A temple? That seems like an unusual place to send a message from."

He shrugged. "It seems unusual to me to send a message to a race we've never heard of for help in rescuing the other Gifted. But a promise is a promise and the sooner we have it fulfilled the happier I'll be."

* * * * *

Pyre and Rayne stood on the street, looking up at the Temple of Nishon. It was an imposing building, made entirely of white stone, carved with detailed frescoes.

"Well," Rayne asked. "Are we just going to stand here or are we going in?"

"I was just thinking . . ."

She waited patiently for him to continue, then prodded him for a response. "You were just thinking what?"

"It's just . . . why a temple? Why not one of the public communications facilities? Who are these Ilezie and why would they want to help us?"

"I don't know. I guess all we can do is trust in the Mother."

He sighed and tried to give her a smile. "I'm sorry. It's just that I'm starting to have some serious doubts about this. Something doesn't seem right but I can't figure out what."

"Are you starting to have premonitions, like the Mother?" she teased.

Pyre shook his head. "No, nothing like that. It's just an uneasy feeling."

She cocked her head, looking at him. "We don't have to go through with this. If you'd rather just go back to the inn . . ."

"No, between the travel here and my illness we've already wasted enough time." He shook his head again but was unable to shake his uneasiness. They really had no choice. "Let's get this over with."

Side by side they climbed the polished steps and entered the open door of the temple. Inside was a small courtyard with several boys with shaven heads, dressed in plain grey robes, sweeping up the debris left from the latest storm. The boys focused intently on their task, ignoring the newcomers.

Pyre reached out and laid his hand on the shoulder of the boy closest to him, stopping him from sweeping. "We are strangers here and require assistance. Where would we go to send a message?"

The boy pointed to a blue door set under an archway.

"Thank you," Pyre told him, releasing him.

The door led to a corridor which had several doors leading off of it. They wandered a few steps forward, then stopped.

"Which way should we go?" Rayne whispered.

"What is it you seek in the temple of Nishon?" a voice asked, startling them. They turned to find a dark robed figure standing behind them. It was impossible to tell whether the figure was male or female. The robe rendered it sexless and a hood was pulled down low over its head.

"I'm not sure we have the right place," Pyre said hesitantly. "We were told to come here to send a message to a race called the Ilezie. Is this possible?"

"This way," the figure told them. It turned and glided back down the corridor.

Pyre and Rayne exchanged a glance and Pyre shrugged slightly. They'd come this far, they might as well see where it ended. They followed after the figure who led them to a brightly lit room where several equally anonymous figures were working at a series of consoles. The contrast of the ancient stone surroundings and the modern equipment was disconcerting.

They passed through this room and into another where three men and two women, priests, no doubt from their shaved heads and white robes, were watching the read-outs that scrolled across three large screens.

"Wait here," their guide told them, and then went over to speak to a priest whose robe was decorated with a wide, gold border around the neck, hem, and ends of the sleeves. The priest listened, nodded, and then spoke in an alien tongue. Everyone else in the room stopped what they were doing and gathered around the central console. A loud hum filled the room as the console powered up.

"What is your message?" their guide asked, returning to them.

Wordlessly, Pyre handed over the envelope he'd been given by the Mother. The envelope hadn't been sealed and before they left the inn Pyre had glanced at the single page of thin parchment. A beautiful, cursive script in black ink filled the page – unfortunately it was a language neither he nor Rayne was familiar with.

The guide handed it over to the priest he'd spoken to and then motioned for them to follow him out of the room. They hesitated, and watched as the envelope was opened and the parchment unfolded. After reading the missive, the priest laid it down and then joined hands with the others around the console.

"Come," their guide said impatiently. "This is not for the eyes of unbelievers."

Filled with misgivings, they followed him out and were led to a small sitting room where they were told to wait. After only a few minutes Pyre began to pace. He didn't like this, not one bit. He kept his thoughts to himself though, not wanting to upset Rayne.

It was almost three hours before their guide returned. "The message has been sent," the figure told them. "You are to return to your lodgings and wait. You will be contacted."

"What? Wait!" Pyre hurried after the guide, who was already moving back up the corridor. "That's it? We just sit around and wait until these Ilezie decide to show up? I don't think you understand what's at stake here."

The guide didn't stop until they were at the blue door again. "The message has been sent," it told them. "Your presence is no longer required. You will be contacted."

"Who's going to contact us and—" Pyre looked around. "Where'd he go?"

Rayne glanced around uneasily. "We've done what we came here to do, let's just go."

"Something's not right," Pyre said. "Does this mean these Ilezie are not of our world? If that's the case, how can they be of any help?"

He felt a sinking feeling in his stomach. This had been a fool's errand. How were they ever going to find the others now?

"Come," Rayne said, pulling at his sleeve. "What's done is done. All we can do now is wait, and trust in the Mother."

Provided the Mother had been in her right mind when she wrote the missive and instructions, Pyre thought. With a sigh he allowed Rayne to lead him back to the entrance.

The first thing Pyre noticed when they stepped through the door was the broom lying on the ground, then the absence of the boys. Before he could push Rayne back through the door again, they were surrounded.

Chapter Fifteen

From Wynne's Journal:
When I was part of the compound, I gave little thought to the world beyond its walls, much less the perimeter fence. But now that I am having to cope with it, on my own, I grow more fearful with each passing day. I do not even know the name of this world, but I do know it is one I would not have chosen for myself. They have a charter in place to keep the communities as agrarian as possible. I can only hope that the village is not too barbaric. My escort to the village sanctuary met me at the appointed place at the appointed time. I must admit I was a nervous wreck while I waited. Twice I thought to turn back, to just lose myself in another village, but the thought of the children would give me strength to go on. Their safety had come at so high a price, and what was the point of saving them if they did not survive the tespiro because their human families did not know what to do. Now I am on the last leg of my journey and there is no turning back.

Though not dressed in uniforms, the men who surrounded them might as well have been. Their dark, ordinary clothing may have been intended to allow them to blend into a crowd, but their military stance, plus the weapons they were carrying, gave them away. It was obvious they were soldiers of some kind, perhaps even the same raiders that had kidnapped the children.

There was pounding and shouting behind the door they had just exited through, but one of the soldiers had already done something to fuse it shut. The two other doors leading from the temple to the courtyard were also fused. The boys who'd been sweeping the courtyard lay in a shadowy corner – hopefully unconscious, not dead.

"We have no quarrel with you," Pyre said with more bravado than he felt. "Let us pass in peace." Their knives, even their walking sticks, were back in the room at the inn. There were five, no, the two who'd dealt with the doors joined them making it seven raiders spread out between them and the exit.

"Stand aside, boy," the one who appeared to be in charge ordered. "All we want is the girl."

"You're the ones who attacked the village, aren't you?" Pyre demanded. "You killed the adults and kidnapped the others. Why?"

Pressure began building in the courtyard, like an electrical charge. It was an involuntary reaction from the two Elementals. A defense mechanism against impending danger.

"It's none of your concern. Just give us the girl and I might let you live."

Rayne stepped closer to Pyre and took his hand. The sky darkened as storm clouds raced. "You might as well shoot us now, I'll never go willing."

The leader flicked a glance upwards. "What are you going to do, girl, give us a good wetting?" he scoffed. "How do you think we found you in the first place? You've led us a merry chase but we knew it was only a matter of time before your lack of control betrayed you. And we don't need you willing." He made a motion with his hand and two of soldiers moved forward.

The tension in the air continued to build. Pyre's eyes filled with flame. Though weak from his illness he was still powerful enough to stop these two. The ground in front of them erupted in a gout of flame.

"Come no closer," he told them. "I have no wish to hurt anyone."

"Another one!" the leader said excitedly. "Careful with them, we need them intact!"

The soldiers fanned out. Rayne let go of Pyre's hand as flames licked over his skin. She closed her eyes and reached out with her mind to the building storm. Drawing as much as she dared on Pyre's energy, she fed it into the storm. A bolt of lightning snaked downwards, impacting on the cobblestones of the courtyard. The men scattered.

"Where's the trank gun?" the leader demanded, taking cover behind one of the stone columns. Another tongue of lightning struck the courtyard, then another. A fourth streaked downwards but with little impact.

"You're running out of steam, girl," the leader called, taking the tranquilizer gun from one of his men.

Pyre drew his arm back and then let loose with a series of fireballs. The raiders cursed and dove for cover again. "C'mon," he told Rayne. "This might be our only chance." Giving the raiders a wide berth, they circled the courtyard, aiming towards the exit. Pyre kept up a steady stream of fireballs but they were losing strength.

"I'm losing control of the storm," Rayne gasped. Her face was frighteningly pale and she was lagging behind. The rain started, big, fat drops at first and then a torrent of water.

Pyre took her hand again, pulling her along with him. They were within a few yards of freedom when he felt a sting in his neck. He slapped the spot and came away with a small flechette in his fingers. A sudden wave of weakness surged through him and he staggered forward, dragging Rayne along with him.

"Just a little further," he said. His limbs started to feel leaden. If they could just make it outside the temple . . . there were plenty of places to hide in the market.

"No!" he cried out as he felt Rayne being wrenched from his grasp. He fought blindly, the rain and the dizziness conspiring to hide his enemies. "Leave us alone!" He could hear Rayne screaming, the men shouting.

"Hold her!"

"I'm trying!"

"Damn it, we weren't prepared for two of them," one of the voices was saying.

Pyre sank to his knees, still swinging. They couldn't have her, Rayne was his! If it took a life time, he would find her again.

"We got what we came for," someone else said. "Let's go."

"What about him? He should be worth a nice bonus."

Pyre felt a hand reach out and try to take a hold of him. Mustering the last of his strength, he sent a wave of heat outwards. With a yelp the man drew his hand back.

"Leave him, it's too dangerous," the leader decided. "We can come back for him another time if we have to."

Whatever drug they'd used, it was potent. Pyre swayed in place. It was hard even to breathe. The rain let up enough that he could see the men leaving the temple, Rayne struggling in their midst. He reached out for her and then fell forward into oblivion.

* * * * *

The rain had stopped by the time the priests were able to get the doors open again. They boiled out of the temple like a swarm of angry ants, but the intruders were gone. Two of them closed and barred the wide outer doors to the courtyard, the others began carrying the unconscious boys into the temple. Four of them gathered around Pyre. They spoke rapidly, in a language he would not have understood had he been conscious.

It was decided to carry him into the temple as well. The first priest to touch him, however, drew back with a gasp of pain. There was more discussion, then one of the priests hurried away.

He returned quickly with one of the white robed archpriests that had been in the main communications room.

"What is the problem?" the archpriest demanded. "Why haven't you brought him into the temple? Our honor—"

"With respect, your eminence, we are unable to move him."

"For this you interrupt us at our task? It is a simple matter to pick him up and—"

Wordlessly, the priest that had reached for him first held up his hands. They were red and blistered. The archpriest took a step forward and frowned.

"It happened when I tried to touch him, your eminence."

The archpriest's breath came out in a hiss. He glanced down at Pyre. "Use a stretcher, and wear leather gloves. He must be protected."

* * * * *

Consciousness came slowly. Pyre stirred and groaned. His head pounded and there was a foul taste in his mouth. It took a great deal of effort to open his eyes and he quickly shut them again as the room began to spin. Sensing he wasn't alone, he forced his eyes open once more and struggled to sit up.

"Where's Rayne?" his voice came out in a raspy cough.

An old woman sat watching him impassively, her white hair unbound and falling past to her waist. When he reached a sitting position she held out a wooden mug. "This will help with the after effects of the tranquilizers."

"Where am I? Why should I trust you?"

"You are in the temple of Nishon. And I suppose you have no reason to trust me other than my assurance I mean you no harm."

Though he had every reason not to trust her, Pyre found that for some reason he did. There was a self-assured calmness about her that was incredibly soothing. He took the mug from her and sipped cautiously. As his head began to clear he studied the woman. Despite the white hair she was not as old as he had first suspected. In fact, she didn't seem much older than he was.

"The priests of Nishon have pledged their aid in recovering your companion. It is a matter of great honor with them. Have you any idea who those men were or what they wanted with you?"

"They came for Rayne," he said slowly. "One of them said that all they wanted was the girl. There was a raid on our village . . . I think they're part of the same group." He felt a dull emptiness inside. Rayne was gone and he had no idea of where to even start looking for her.

"Maybe you should start at the beginning," she said gently.

Pyre looked at her dispiritedly. His trust only went so far. She was a stranger and he was a keeper of many secrets. How much should he tell her? Although he'd lived apart from the village he had been secure in the knowledge it was there. Now he was the only one left.

"There is not much to tell," he said at last. "There was a raid on our village, the adults were killed and the Gi— the children kidnapped. Rayne and I escaped only because we were not there at the time."

"I was not aware that raiders were a problem on this world."

"They are not. Our village is isolated, even more so than most." Pyre could feel his fire begin to build and worked to calm himself down again. The last thing he needed to do was to lose control. "I have no idea why any one would do such a thing."

"Do you not? And yet you travelled such a long way to the temple of Nishon, specifically to send a message to the Ilezie to petition for aid."

He froze, mug half way to his mouth.

"The question is, whose idea was it to send this message, yours or your companion's? Or was it someone else's?"

Pyre's mind worked frantically, trying to come up with a plausible explanation that would not betray his family and friends.

"Perhaps an even better question would be, how does an Ardraci with such power end up on a farming world, and how is it that you've reached such an age and yet have so little control of your element?"

Chapter Sixteen

From Wynne's Journal:

It took five more days to reach the village sanctuary. I expressed my amazement at how much work has been done in so short a time, and was told that the building of this sanctuary was started just after I first met with the humans on a regular basis. It appears there is more to these humans than we first realized. There are so many more children here than I had expected. In the night as I lay in my bed in the cottage the villagers built me, I start to panic thinking of all that lies ahead. Teaching them control, guiding them through their tespiro. These aren't just children, they're Elementals, genetically enhanced Elementals. Only time will tell how Dr. Arjun's experiments have affected them. Only time will tell if I've done more harm than good in liberating them.

The blood drained from Pyre's face. "I don't understand." He didn't know what an Ardraci was, but she knew about his element. How was this possible? The gifts were never talked about to outsiders, it was a secret the whole village kept. Pale flames licked across his skin. Though his energy was greatly depleted he believed he could still muster enough fire to escape.

From out of nowhere a breeze sprang up, dousing his flame. His eyes widened. The woman cocked her head, looking at him curiously. "Why are you so afraid?"

"Who are you?" he whispered.

"I am Nakeisha Windsinger, Ardraci representative and designated liaison for the Ilezie to the Pan-Galactic Council. And you would be . . . ?"

"P-P-Pyrphoros," he stuttered.

"Well, Pyrphoros. Now that we have been properly introduced, perhaps you could tell me why I am here."

He stared at her helplessly.

"In all fairness I must tell you, the priests of Nishon did not wish to keep you sedated until I arrived, but they had no choice."

"Sedated?" he repeated, totally confused. Why would the priests feel the need to do this? They'd been only too happy to shove him and Rayne out their doors once the Mother's message was sent. Why keep him now?"

"You lost control of your element," she said gently. "Even now you can barely keep your fire under control."

"How do you know this?" he burst out.

Her eyebrows raised. "I told you, I am Ardraci as well. My gift is the Wind." The breeze returned, circling him twice, drying the sweat that had broken out on his forehead.

"But . . . you are not from the village!"

"You mentioned a village . . . was the entire village Ardraci?"

"What is Ardraci?"

It was her turn for confusion. "It is the world we all come from."

"I don't know what you mean. I came from the village. We all did."

"Oh, this is not good," she said. "This is not good at all. Tell me, Pyrphoros, was everyone in your village an Elemental?"

He shook his head slowly. "No, not everyone, just the Gifted. And we were never to show our gifts or speak of them outside of the village."

She sat back in her chair and rubbed her forehead. "So how did these raiders know about the elemental gifts?" she muttered. "And for what purpose would they take them?" She sighed heavily. "How old were these Gifted?"

"They ranged in age from ten to twenty-three. I was the oldest at twenty-five."

"And did they all lack control of their elements?" She seemed to be trying to grasp a hold of the idea.

"The Mother tried her best to teach us, but . . ."

"The Mother? Was she taken too?"

Pyre shook his head. "No, she lived apart from the village, as did I. The raiders did not find her cottage. But she was ill and Rayne and I could not help her – she returned to her element."

"I am sorry for your loss," she said quietly. She studied him as she considered everything he'd told her so far. "And you have no idea who these raiders might be?"

He shook his head. "We were a peaceful village, few knew we even existed."

The woman sighed in frustration.

"Wait. There was something . . ." He sat up a little straighter. "The raiders had others with gifts who aided them."

"Others with elemental powers?"

"Yes! The Mother said he had true Elementals who learned to work together. Water and Air to make snow."

"Water and Air," she mused. "I have heard legends of this, but it is very rare. Who is this "he" you mentioned?"

"We don't know," he said with regret. "The Mother died before she could tell us."

"You have set me quite the mystery to solve, my friend, but our first priority needs be rescuing these

Gifted, and your friend," she added when he looked like he was about to protest.

"There is a book," he said suddenly. "The Mother left us a book that we were to give to the Ilezie."

"Where is this book?"

"It's at the inn, where Rayne and I had a room. If I could go back there . . ."

"No need," she assured him. "After the attack on the Temple, the priests decided it would be best if you stayed here. They had your things brought here for safe keeping." With a sweep of her hand she indicated the tall cupboard beside the bed.

Pyre looked inside and found his and Rayne's packs as well as their walking sticks and bedrolls. He rummaged around in his pack and withdrew the leather bound book, still tied with its knotted cord. He held it in his hands and looked at the woman sitting near him.

"If you would prefer to wait for the Ilezie to arrive, I understand," she said quietly. "But this book might contain some of the answers we are looking for and knowledge can be a powerful weapon."

Without a word, he passed her the book then lay back down on the bed while she began to read.

Nakeisha turned another page of the diary and glanced at the man lying on the bed. She felt only slightly guilty for lacing his tea with a sedative, but he needed to be kept calm and the sedative was easier on him than the tranquilizers the priests had used.

"Do you know what is in this?" she asked.

Pyre kept his eyes closed and shook his head. "No, the Mother asked us to deliver it to the Ilezie, we did not believe it was for our eyes." He felt a strange lassitude, as though he was wrapped in a soft cloud.

"Does the name Dr. Arjun mean anything to you?"

"No, should it?"

She sighed heavily. "I suppose not. This Mother, was she the only adult that was gifted?"

"I . . ." Pyre struggled to sit up on the bed again. "Yes, she was." There was a slightly bewildered look on his face as he continued. "How is this possible? How can the children have gifts but the parents not?"

"I think you already know the answer to that," she said softly, face full of compassion.

"They were not our real parents," he said slowly. He didn't remember his birth parents, his foster-mother had taken him in when they were killed in a rock fall. At least that is what he'd always been told.

"Your companion, Rayne. Her gift is Water, is it not?"

"Yes," he said warily.

"Was she responsible for the storms the priests have told me of?"

Here he hesitated, long years of keeping the village secrets coming to the fore.

"It is all right," she told him. "But it is most likely how these raiders were able to find you. I believe if we find your companion we will find the others as well."

Pyre sat up straighter as her words registered. "Then you'll help?"

She looked at him in surprise. "But of course. How could I not? We are of the same people, no matter that you were not born on Ardraci."

"Where do we start?" he asked. He stood up and immediately swayed in place, forcing him to sit down again.

"Easy, my friend," she smiled at his eagerness. "You've been asleep for three days, your body will need time to recover—"

"Three days!" he repeated, appalled. They'd never be able to track the raiders through the city after three days.

"Be at ease, the priests have not lain idle. They know which way the raiders went and have sent their information to my ship."

"Ship?" he repeated stupidly. Of course she'd have a ship, how else could she have got here. It was just a lot to take in all at once.

"You have been through a great deal, Pyrphoros —"

"Pyre," he said suddenly.

"I beg your pardon?"

"My name. I prefer to be called Pyre."

She smiled. "I thank you for the gift of your name. I will have the priests escort us to my ship and —"

"Priests?" he scoffed. "What good would priests do if the raiders return?"

Arching an eyebrow, she asked, "Have you not wondered why the raiders felt the need to lock the priests in their temple when they kidnapped your companion?"

He shook his head. From his point of view he thought it had more to do with keeping him and Rayne from escaping back into the temple than keeping the priests trapped. What kind of resistance could priests make?

"The warrior-priests of Nishon are well known for their fighting skills, you would do well to remember this. I suspect we will need their aid before this is done."

Pyre shifted, wanted to argue the point, but simply nodded instead.

"You have been through a great deal, Pyre," she said gently. "There are none who would think any less of you should you decide to stay here, in the temple."

Was she really implying he should hide like a coward while Rayne was in who knew what kind of danger? He stood again, and this time he pushed the dizziness aside, standing straight and steady. "You will not leave me behind."

She nodded, unsurprised. "So be it."

Chapter Seventeen

From Wynne's Journal:
The children thrive and the humans are happy. The vil-
lage, though remote, is prosperous. While the children are so
young there is really not much I can help their parents with,
other than advice in my capacity as a former medical technician
and mid-wife. At this stage all I can do is re-enforce the need
for secrecy. I have no sense of foreboding, but still, there are mis-
givings, as of something I am missing . . . Any thoughts I may
have ever harbored of contacting the home world or the Ilezie
have been made impossible. There has been something bothering
me regarding the children and I have finally realized what it is.
It is their growth rates. Over a third of them are developing at
an accelerated rate, most likely a result of the growth hormones
their parents were given. Was this planned by Dr. Arjun? I
will probably never know the answer.

Rayne paced within the confines of her cell. Oh,
it may have been made to look like a bedroom —
wooden bedstead with matching table and dresser,

bright woven rug on the floor, walls with a cheerful floral paper over them – but she knew it was a cell. There was no window behind the yellow curtains, the door to the sanitary facilities didn't lock, and the only door into the room did . . . from the outside.

They'd been sent for her specifically, but why just her and not Pyre? If this had something to do with their gifts, as she was beginning to suspect, then they should have taken him too. His gift was far more powerful than hers.

Her heart had nearly stopped, seeing Pyre fall. She struggled to go to him but creating the storm had weakened her considerably, even after siphoning energy from him. It had been instinctive, drawing on his power. It was her fault he succumbed so easily – she stole his energy and left him defenseless.

Then one of the raiders stabbed her with something and things grew vague after that. She'd been dragged through the deserted market and tied to a horse, that much she remembered. But she had no idea what direction they'd taken. It had taken two days for them to reach this place, wherever this place was. She'd spent most of that that time in a drug-induced haze.

Her next clear memory was arriving at a stockade built against a rocky cliff. There'd been something odd about buildings inside the stockade, but she blacked out again before she could figure it out.

When she awoke again, it was to find herself locked in this room.

With a sigh she sat down on the bed, wrapping her arms around her legs and resting her chin on her knees. They brought her food, but none of her guards would talk to her. Had they gone back for Pyre as well? She had no way of knowing.

The rasp of a key in a lock had her looking towards the door. One of the guards opened it but instead of a second guard with a tray, there was an elderly man in a white coat with an electronic pad in his hand.

"Well, my dear. You've lead us a merry chase, but you're safely here now. I hope you find your accommodations to your satisfaction." He beamed at her in a fatherly way. An involuntary shiver went up her spine.

Rayne lowered her feet to the floor, but otherwise stayed sitting on the bed. "Who are you? Why have you brought me here? Where *is* here?"

"Tsk! So many questions." He consulted the pad. "Your primary element is water, but there's something else coming through in your readings. What else can you do, my dear?"

"W—w—what do you mean?"

"Come now, don't play coy. We ran a full medical scan on you when you arrived."

A medical scan. The Mother had mentioned something about a medical scanner once when she was teaching her healing. "Such devices are forbidden by the charter," she blurted out.

"The charter does not apply to me," he stated, his fatherly façade slipping. "I did not come to this world as a settler, I was forced here by circumstances." He paced to one side of the room and back again. "You might as well tell me," he said. "I'll find out sooner or later."

Rayne made no comment. This man, whoever he was, frightened her, though she couldn't say why.

"What is it about you subjects from the village that makes you so repressed when it comes to your elements?" he muttered.

"Are the others from the village here as well?" she asked, unable to help herself.

"Where else would they be?" he asked irritably. "Tell me about this young man you were with. A Fire Elemental, was he not? I don't appear to have a record for him."

"A record?"

"All the results from my breeding program are recorded." He shook his head in amusement. "They were fools to believe I didn't know what was going on. They were just lucky the breeders who died were near the end of their usefulness. Now, about the record for this Fire Elemental . . ."

"I don't understand." Her eyes tracked him as he continually moved around the room.

"A record, prior knowledge. Your scan didn't show you as one of the accelerated children, I would expect your mental faculties to be far more advanced."

"There's nothing wrong with the minds of the twice-gifted. They just need kindness and understanding." They were gentle souls, adult in body but childlike in mind, their growth rate was so swift their minds could not keep pace.

"What they needed was to be put down," he said harshly. "They were an accident. Totally useless for my purpose."

"What do you mean?" she asked in dawning horror.

"I mean, they have been disposed of, like they should have been from the beginning. You need not worry about them any longer."

"Who are you?" she whispered.

"My name is Dr. Arjun. I'm your creator."

Rayne stared at the man in front of her. He couldn't possibly mean what she thought he did when he said the twice-gifted had been disposed of . . . could he?

"You k-k-killed them? You murdered those innocent children, like you did our parents?"

"Not children," he said with distaste, "Accidents. Had they remained in the lab they would have been destroyed at birth. And those villagers weren't your parents. They were no relation to you at all."

"Then why kill them!"

He raised an eyebrow. "They left me no choice. I needed a new influx of DNA and they were standing in my way."

"Of course they stood in your way, you were trying to kidnap their children!"

"Not their children, mine. I can see you are woefully ignorant of your true purpose," he said, shaking his head. "You were born as part of my breeding program and you exist only to further that program."

"Breeding program?" she repeated, appalled. "We're people, not livestock."

"Oh, but that's where you're wrong, my dear," he told her. "You are livestock, my livestock, even though I allowed you to be raised outside of this compound. And once I've assessed the strength of your ability, you will be bred as I see fit."

"You're insane; I won't have any part of this!"

He laughed. "What makes you think I'm giving you a choice?"

Dread crawled up her spine, making her shiver. She stared at him with wide eyes, unable to speak.

"Now, I suggest you rest up. You have a full day of testing tomorrow." He rapped his knuckles on the door and the guard let him out, locking the door behind him.

* * * * *

Pyre paced back and forth in the room he'd been given on the ship. Waiting and more waiting, he was sick of all this waiting. He needed action. He needed to find Rayne and the others from the village. Flames licked across his fingertips.

The chime of his door sounded and he spun in his tracks. "Come in," he called.

Nakeisha entered, together with two other beings. The first was a tall, lean, man with burnished skin and white hair. The other was shorter, thinner, and enveloped in a hooded robe of grayish brown.

"Why are we just sitting here?" Pyre said before he could stop himself. "We need to get moving before the trail grows any colder."

"I understand your anxiety, my friend," Nakeisha said. "But you must understand that these were not simple raiders who have taken your friends."

"What do you mean?" He could feel his fire crackling just below his skin and worked hard to keep it under control.

"Perhaps we should sit for the telling of this tale."

He bit back a sharp retort and nodded. Sitting down to listen never boded well. He had a bad feeling about what she was going to tell him. The smaller being seemed to be staring at him and after a moment he realized his fire was waning.

"Pyre, may I introduce my *enjulla*, Chaney, and our dear friend E.Z." Nakeisha said. "They—"

"How did you do that?" he asked.

Nakeisha looked startled. "How did I do—"

"Not you, him." He pointed at the hooded figure. "How did you dissipate my fire?"

"A simple matter, for someone who knows what they're doing." The figure turned to Nakeisha. "You were right about his control, or lack thereof. It is a miracle he has reached such an age."

"What—"

The figure turned back to Pyre. "Have you had any training at all in your element?"

"No, I—"

"With a gift as powerful as yours, you have done well on your own. But if you are to come with us when we rescue your friends you will need to have better control of your element."

"Who are you?"

The being lowered the hood of his robe. "My name is Elea'zaregaheherneinar. I am of the Ilezie."

Chapter Eighteen

From Wynne's Journal:
It would have been foolish to believe that the parents of the children would remain in ignorance for long. Eventually several of them approached me and I could do nothing but tell them the truth. I despaired, at first, of being able to explain what was happening without becoming too technical, however I had forgotten these people were not always the simple folk they appeared to be. Though some were second and third generation settlers, all of them had some understanding of science and genetics. The children grow and thrive and seem well-adjusted. They do not appear to be bothered by the discrepancies in growth rates but accept it as just the way things are. Of course they know no other life so they have nothing to compare it to. The only worries the adults have is whether or not the accelerated growth rate will eventually slow as the children reach maturity or whether the af-

fected children will continue to age rapidly. Unfortunately, I have no answers to give them. Only time will tell.

Pyre studied the creature standing before him. This was the creature that the Mother was so in awe of? This was the Ilezie that was going to rescue the children? It didn't look like much – small and thin, almost delicate looking, it had pale, luminous violet skin and large golden eyes. It stared at him as though expecting some kind of reaction.

"What are the Ilezie going to do to find the children?" he demanded. "And what do you mean, *if* I am to go with you?"

Clearly this was not what the creature was expecting. Blue, then green, pigment chased across its skin before settling back to violet. Nakeisha smothered a grin.

"You do seem to have a one-track mind, don't you?" E.Z. said mildly. He didn't move, yet somehow he seemed suddenly larger, more menacing. Pyre fell back a step, yet still E.Z.'s presence seemed to grow.

"The man who has your friends is known to us," he said in a voice that seemed to fill every corner of the room. "Now sit down and listen."

Pyre sat. He noticed from the corner of his eye that Nakeisha and Chaney sat as well.

"Now, there are things you need to know before we begin," E.Z. continued. The room suddenly lightened as the enormous presence vanished and he became nothing more than a small, delicate creature again. He sighed heavily and began to pace.

"Nakeisha has explained to you that you, none of you, belong to this world. Yes?"

Pyre nodded. It was one of the few things she explained that actually made sense.

"Many years before any of you were born, there was a group of geneticists on Ardraci who started experimenting with the elemental genome. The reasons don't matter now, what matters is they had to be stopped. Unfortunately, one of them, Uri Arjun, had an almost cult-like following. He and his followers escaped from Ardraci. Four of his ships were retrieved but the fifth, the one with Arjun on it, disappeared."

"Arjun, you mentioned that name," Pyre said to Nakeisha.

"Yes, it was mentioned in the journal you gave me."

"Arjun made it as far as this world, where he continued with his genetic experimentation."

"Wait, you're saying we were born from these experiments?" Pyre asked, appalled.

E.Z. stopped and stood before him. "Yes, that's exactly what I'm saying. Wynne Ignitus, the woman you knew as The Mother, worked for Dr. Arjun until she could no longer bear to take part in his madness. She began smuggling infants from the labs, finding sympathetic humans to place them with."

"Our parents," Pyre said.

"We can only assume."

"If she felt that strongly about what this doctor was doing, why didn't she contact the Ilezie back then?"

E.Z. and Nakeisha exchanged a look.

"In the beginning Arjun's objective was to create a better, more powerful Elemental. But later that goal became perverted. He began trying to isolate specific aspects of an element and splice two or more elements into a single entity."

"And we, all of us from the village, are the product of these experiments?" Pyre guessed. His mind was reeling. His whole life was a lie; all their lives were.

"As are those who were *not* rescued as infants. As for why Wynne was reluctant to contact us . . ." here E.Z. hesitated.

"She had been away from the home world for a long time," Nakeisha said gently.

Pyre looked from one to the other. There was something he was missing. Some undercurrent he couldn't quite grasp.

"What aren't you telling me?"

"She was probably afraid of how the Ilezie would react to the children," Chaney, who'd been quiet up until now, broke in. Nakeisha shot him a quelling look.

"The Ardraci are special to the Ilezie and I fear she forgot this," Nakeisha said. "She was probably afraid of what their reaction to the breeding program would be."

"Afraid of their reaction? But what—" he stopped suddenly as the truth dawned on him. "She was afraid they'd do something to us, wasn't she?"

Their silence was all the answer he needed.

Pyre looked from one to the other of the three people in the room with him, his gaze settling on the Ilezie. "Is this true? Was the Mother, Wynne, afraid of what the Ilezie would do to us once they found out we were the result of a breeding program?"

"I cannot presume to know what was in Wynne's mind," E.Z. said, a little stiffly.

He was so obviously uncomfortable discussing this that Pyre jumped to the most logical conclusion. "You would save the children from being used by this Dr. Arjun, only to destroy them yourselves?"

"No! Never!"

He looked genuinely appalled, but Pyre had spent too many years keeping secrets to be so easily convinced. Nakeisha looked equally upset at the idea, but Chaney looked thoughtful.

"I understand why you'd think that—" he held up a hand as Nakeisha and E.Z. started to protest. "Hear me out." He turned back to Pyre. "You, all of you, were taught at an early age to hide what you are, is this not so?"

"That's right," Pyre agreed cautiously.

"Were you ever told *why* you must keep others from learning of your gifts?"

"I don't . . . no, not really. Just that others wouldn't understand."

Chaney nodded. "And that made you different. It made you feel as though you were somehow . . . wrong."

"Yes," Pyre whispered.

"Well you are not," Chaney said forcefully. "No more than my beloved is 'wrong' or our children are wrong."

"You have children?"

"Twins," Chaney said with a grin at the younger man's surprise. "We have yet to determine what Shinandu's gift is, but Kandor is an entirely new element – much as some of your friends may be. And woe to anyone, Ilezie or not, who tries to harm them."

"The Ilezie knew from conception that Kandor would be different. If we had any notion of interfering, we would have done so then."

Nakeisha turned to E.Z. "What would you have done?"

He looked faintly surprised. "Why, nothing. It is not our way to interfere with the natural progression of life. What Uri Arjun is doing, however, is most unnatural. The children resulting from his experiments will be given the same choice all Ardraci are given, but still cherished as all children should be."

"What do you mean, the same choice?"

"While all Elementals are Ardraci, not all Ardraci become Elementals," Nakeisha told him. "You are given the choice before entering *tespiro* to either accept your gift and become a full Elemental, or reject your gift and have it blocked. If you wish to accept your gift, you are given training to learn to control it."

"Why were we not given this choice?" Pyre asked. He knew several gifted that he'd grown up with who would have gladly given up their gifts.

"Because only with the help of an Ilezie can a gift be successfully blocked," E.Z. told him. "It takes a great amount of skill and power to block a gift. The greater the gift, the harder it is to block."

"The choice is given before *tespiro*," Pyre said. "What about after, can a gift be blocked after?"

Here E.Z. hesitated. "To my knowledge it has never been done. If there were a compelling reason it could be attempted, but it would be dangerous, very dangerous, to both the Ilezie and the Elemental."

Pyre nodded thoughtfully. "You said I needed to control my element if I am to go with you to rescue the others. Can you help me with that?"

"Yes."

"What must I do?"

"I can transfer the knowledge directly into your mind, but it will be up to you to be able to use it. I must warn you," he said, looking Pyre in the eye, "this could be dangerous to both us both."

"I'm willing to take the risk if you are," Pyre told him. He just hoped he wouldn't regret his decision.

Chapter Nineteen

From Wynne's Journal:

My heart is sorely wounded. I have lost one of the children and though it was through no fault of my own, I still feel his loss keenly. His name was Gyges, he was of the earth. He'd been out in the woods with some other boys, playing as healthy, happy children are wont to do, when he fell and cut his leg on a jagged piece of metal. It was badly infected before his parents thought to consult me. Perhaps if he had been brought to me sooner . . . but in any case there was little I could do besides ease his return to the Earth. Thank the powers the children are a healthy lot. I don't know what I'd do if they became ill — childhood illness can often bring on an early tespiro, which is the last thing I need. I am still uncertain how I am to handle their normal tespiro when the time comes without trained professionals to aid me. All I know is I do not want to ever face another such loss.

Pyre looked around uneasily. He did not like being back in the courtyard of the temple, but E.Z. insisted that the transfer of knowledge would be safest if done outdoors. The outer doors of the courtyard were locked. Pyre and E.Z. sat facing each other in the center, a smoky glass sphere on a stand in between them. A ring of priests surrounded them, facing outwards.

"This orb is the conduit through which knowledge may be shared," E.Z. told Pyre.

"How does it work?"

"You need only to place your hands on it. I will do the rest."

Hesitantly, Pyre reached out and placed his hands on the sphere. It was warm, not cold as he'd expected. The cloud within it swirled and changed from smoky white to silvery-grey, then swirled faster and brightened as E.Z. laid his hands on it as well. The surface of it began to heat quickly. Pyre automatically tried to pull away but found he couldn't. His hands were stuck fast to the sphere.

As he opened his mouth to protest, the pain hit. It started in his hands and then traveled up his arms to the rest of him until every nerve ending was on fire. His mouth was frozen open. The pain took his breath away. A low humming filled his head, building in intensity.

Are you ready? E.Z. asked in his mind.

He wanted to say no, that he changed his mind, but the word that formed was, *Yes*.

If Pyre thought the pain was bad before, it was nothing compared to what he was feeling now. It was as though a hand was rifling through his thoughts. His soul was laid bare to the Ilezie – there were no secrets, no awareness of self, there was only the pain and the alien hand sifting through his psyche.

When it was over, the pain left so abruptly he keeled over. Dimly he was aware of the priests breaking formation. Footsteps approached and Nakeisha gently helped him to sit up again.

"You tested him!" she said to E.Z., accusation in her voice.

"Every Elemental is tested, you know this."

"You might have warned him!"

"Were you warned?"

She appeared to have no answer to this. Pyre wished they would both just shut up. His head pounded, although it hurt less with every passing second. "I'm fine," he assured her. "Really I am. In fact—" His eyes widened. "I'm better than fine. All this knowledge . . ."

He held out a hand and conjured a flame that danced from fingertip to fingertip. "It's all so easy, once you understand," he said in wonder.

"You have the knowledge now," E.Z. agreed, "But you must practice to learn how to use it."

Nakeisha stared at E.Z. "All those years I struggled with control . . . you could have helped me and you didn't?"

"And what lesson would you have learned from that?"

Still she stared at him, refusing to be mollified.

"In Pyre's case we have his age and strength to consider, plus we are under a time constraint."

"How strong is he?" she asked quietly.

E.Z. looked faintly troubled. "I have never seen his equal. Yet for all that, he was not the One."

"What one?" Pyre asked, puzzled. The pain in his head had faded and he was starting to deal with his new-found knowledge.

"The One who was foretold," E.Z. said. He sighed. "The Ilezie have a symbiotic relationship to the home world. It was foretold long ago there would come a time when that bond would be threatened, but there would be One among the Ardraci who would save us."

Chaney looked at E.Z. thoughtfully. "Do you think it's possible that Dr. Arjun was conducting his experiments to try and create this One?"

"The thought had crossed my mind," E.Z. admitted. "But it would mean he had aid from one of my brethren. As much as we all seek the One, to do so in this fashion is . . . immoral."

Pyre had had enough talking. "I'm perfectly fine now," he said, getting to his feet. "When can we get going?"

"So impatient, you remind me of someone else," E.Z. said, eyes flicking towards Nakeisha. "Very well, there is plenty of daylight remaining. Provisions have been gathered and a route has been plotted out. As our young friend has rightly pointed out, it is time to go."

"Wait," Pyre said. "It's just the four of us against who knows how many raiders?"

"Not just the four of us. Look behind you."

Pyre turned around. There were at least a dozen priests standing in the courtyard. They'd left their robes behind and were dressed head to toe in close fitting black. Even their heads and most of their faces were covered. Though they did not appear to be carrying any weapons, they looked quite formidable.

"Well then," Chaney said, shouldering a pack Pyre hadn't noticed before. "Let's go rescue some children."

* * * * *

Rayne lay curled up in desolation on the bed in her room. The tests had been embarrassing and intrusive, some of them even painful. The people who'd subjected them to her had been cold and impersonal. They made her feel like an object, not a real person.

A sob caught in her throat. She missed Pyre. She missed his gentleness, the sound of his voice. She even missed his volatile anger. She wished she'd never persuaded him to fulfill the Mother's last request – they could have gone back up the mountain to his cave and lived in peace for the rest of their lives. Was he safe? Was he thinking of her? The strangers in the laboratory refused to answer any of her questions.

Before she could lose herself in her misery, she heard the sound of her door being unlocked. Rayne stiffened, but otherwise didn't move. No more tests. She couldn't bear it if they took her back to that room. She'd fight them with everything she had.

There was a click of the door being shut again, but there was also a whisper of movement. Someone was in the room with her. She flinched and rolled away from the contact as there was a hesitant touch on her arm.

"I'm sorry," a quiet, masculine voice said. "I didn't mean to startle you. I just . . . are you all right?"

"All right? All right?" Rayne had trouble controlling her volume as she uncurled herself and sat up. "I've been kidnapped and held against my will, I've been poked and prodded within an inch of my life, and some lunatic has told me I'm going to be used in some kind of breeding program. What makes you think I'd be all right?" She stared at the young man who'd backed a few steps away from her. "Who are you?"

He was tall, almost as tall as Pyre but more heavily set. His blond hair was short and straight, his eyes a pale blue. There was something strangely familiar about him, though she'd never seen him before. He was dressed in the same dark blue tunic and drawstring pants she was wearing. They'd taken her own clothes away from her during the testing. There was something else about him and she finally figured out what it was.

"You're Gifted like me, aren't you?" she asked. "Your gift is Water."

He smiled tentatively at her, but kept his distance. "That's right, I'm a third generation Water Elemental. My name is Kairavini, but you can call me Ravi if you like."

Rayne frowned. "What do you mean, third generation?"

"I think you know what I mean. My parents, and their parents before them, were all Water Elementals."

"You're part of this breeding program, aren't you?" she whispered, appalled. She moved to the other side of the bed, putting it between them. "Is that why you're here? I'm warning you right now, I have no intention of creating a fourth generation with you."

"Relax, that's not why I'm here. I just thought—" He sighed and ran a hand through his hair. "I'm not supposed to be here. I just thought you might be needing a friend."

"A friend?" she repeated, voice laced with suspicion. "Is that what you are?"

"I could be. At the very least I can try and answer some of your questions. Look, do you mind if I sit down?"

She shrugged and watched warily as he sat down in one of the chairs. He seemed sincere, but she was not about to give her trust so easily. "All right, friend, you say you can answer my questions so answer me this, how do I get out of here?"

Ravi shook his head, genuine regret filling his eyes. "I don't know." When she opened her mouth to protest he held up his hands. "Honestly, I don't. There are five restricted areas and the way out of the compound is through one of them. I don't know which one. I've never been to the outside."

"You've never been outside of this place?" she asked, horrified. "You've never seen the grass or the trees, never seen the sky at night, filled with stars?"

"I was born and raised in the compound. Some day, when my usefulness is over, I'll die here."

"How can you be so offhand about it?" She couldn't imagine never having felt the sun warm her skin, or the wind in her face; to never have stood under the rain as it rejuvenated the earth.

He shrugged. "I can't miss what I've never had. This is all I've ever known."

Chapter Twenty

From Wynne's Journal:
Though I have no child of my own, the villagers have taken to calling me Mother. I suppose it's as good a name as any. I am set apart from the others both by the distance my cottage is from the village, and the knowledge I have. I still struggle with my place in such an agrarian society. The villagers look to me as a leader. I find this ironic for despite my role in the escape with the children, I have always been a follower, not a leader. Perhaps it is because I have no family ties and can be neutral when settling disputes. I find myself in a quandary. Do I teach the children how to use their gifts or how to suppress them? One can be just as dangerous as the other. I have impressed upon the parents the need for secrecy; now that the children are maturing we need to impress the need on them as well.

Using their gifts could lead to discovery, but not using them could lead to an out of control element. They have been raised with such love and care . . . I fear for them in the outside world

Rayne stared at the young man sitting in the chair in front of her, fighting a wave of pity. She didn't want to feel sorry for him; she didn't want to make a friend. She wanted to get out of here, to feel Pyre's arms around her again. She missed him so much she ached.

They stared at each other for a few minutes until Rayne couldn't stand it any longer. "How many others with the water gift are there?"

Ravi shrugged. "Nine, ten counting you. But only three others are pure water."

"What do you mean, pure water?"

"I mean their parents were both water as well. There are only a few pure Elementals left. Of course there are many others that have been crossed with water."

Rayne shuddered. It all sounded so cold, so calculated. "What about your parents?"

"What about them?" he asked in surprise.

"How can they let this happen?"

"They don't have a choice."

"But don't you talk to them about it?"

"There's no one to talk to," he told her. "Men are kept in a different section of the compound. Children are kept with their mothers for the first two years, then transferred to the nursery until they reach *tespiro*. If they survive, they're given their own rooms."

"That's horrible!" The words were out before she could stop them. Rayne couldn't imagine the kind of life Ravi lived. "What about siblings? How do you know if someone else is a brother or sister or just a friend?"

"Breeding is strictly controlled. Cross-breeding between siblings would result in genetic degradation. As for friends . . . we aren't really encouraged to socialize – it's too tempting to form attachments and that's strictly forbidden."

"Why?"

"It makes it too hard if you get attached to the wrong person," he said quietly.

"I don't understand."

"Are you really as naïve as you seem?"

"Feel free to leave my room any time," Rayne said frostily.

"I'm sorry, I—" He sighed and scraped his hand through his hair. "Say you make friends with someone and he cares deeply for a woman. But when it comes time for her to be bred you're chosen instead of him. What would that do to your friendship? And worse, what if she had feelings for him as well?" He shook his head. "No, it would just make things so much worse."

"But surely if the two they wish to b-b-breed do not care for each other . . ." Rayne swallowed hard.

She was raised on a farm, she knew what was done with reluctant animals. "There are artificial means to do so."

"Dr. Arjun believes he gets better results with the old fashioned method."

"But . . ." Rayne had a hard time choosing the right words. "What if you refuse? Surely they can't force . . ."

He shivered slightly and looked at her bleakly. "Trust me, they can."

Rayne believed him. They lapsed into silence again.

"If socializing is discouraged," Rayne said finally, "How were you able to come here?"

Ravi brightened, grateful for the change in topic. "They're a little short on guards right now, and Arjun's in an unusually good mood. One of the new people that were brought in is a Fire Elemental."

Rayne straightened up. "That's my sister! What have they done to her?"

"Relax, she's fine! Fire Elementals are rare; they won't let anything happen to her. They'll take very good care of her."

"And then they'll breed her, like she's some kind of animal," she said bitterly.

"Not right away, she hasn't been through her *tespiro* yet."

"How soon?"

"How soon after her *tespiro*? A year, maybe more. It depends on whether or not he finds a suitable . . . partner."

He stopped suddenly, but Rayne had the feeling he had more to say. "What? What is it?"

"It's nothing."

"Tell me!"

"It's just . . . Dr. Arjun. I've heard that his element is fire."

Rayne stared at her visitor, the blood leaving her face. "My sister, and th-th-that old man? But that's—no! I won't let that happen!"

There was pity in his eyes as he looked at her. "There won't be anything you can do to stop it if that's what he decides. I'm sorry. I didn't mean to upset you. He's probably too old to make a viable candidate."

She continued to stare at him, horror filling her eyes.

"I should probably leave before I'm missed." He rose to his feet and went to the door where he stopped. "I shouldn't have come here. I'm sorry."

"Why did you come?"

"I overheard some of the technicians talking about the new subjects that were brought in and the hard time they were having adjusting to the compound. I thought . . . I just thought I could help put you at your ease. I think I've only made things worse for you and for that I truly am sorry."

He stood for a moment as though waiting for her to speak and when she didn't he slipped through the door. Rayne heard the lock click into place as the door shut behind him.

Oh, Pyre, she called in her mind. *Where are you? You need to save us, to save me, before it's too late.*

* * * * *

Pyre jerked upright from where he was dozing beside the campfire. This had been their first full day of travelling but he was too keyed up to sleep. Rayne was never far from his thoughts. He wondered what was happening to her, if she was all right.

"What is it?" Chaney asked in a low voice. He was the only other one awake, aside from the sentries the priests had insisted on posting.

"I—it's nothing," Pyre's face was slightly flushed by the light of the dying fire.

Chaney looked at him steadily and Pyre sighed. "It's just . . . I fear for Rayne. She is so much in my mind that for a moment I thought I heard her call out to me."

"Perhaps you did."

Pyre shook his head. "No matter how much I wish it could be, I fear it is impossible."

"Is it? In the last two years I've learned very little is impossible when it comes to the Ilezie, or the Ardraci. Nakeisha and I share a mind bond, many mated Ardraci are able to do so."

"But . . . you are not Ardraci."

"No, I'm not. But I'm mated to one, and a very powerful one at that."

"Rayne and I are not mated, we have only been together a short time."

"But you've shared her bed, am I correct?" The deepening flush on Pyre's face gave Chaney his answer. "When the pairing is right, a bond can be formed early in a relationship. You should talk to E.Z. about it."

Pyre nodded. "It would make my mind easy, to know that she's come to no harm."

"I'm sure it would. Now, we should try and get some sleep. The archpriest said that if we really push it, we can reach Dr. Arjun's compound by the end of the day."

In the morning, Pyre hesitantly approached E.Z., whom he'd been avoiding since the sharing of their minds that gave him control of his element. While he didn't exactly fear the Ilezie, the experience left him with a healthy dose of respect for the creature. And creature the Ilezie was. For all its humanoid appearance there was nothing human about the mind that had rifled through his.

"I would beg a favor," he said hesitantly, still too much in awe of the delicate looking Ilezie to be at ease with him.

"And I would grant your favor, should I be able to do so. Please, sit down and tell me what it is."

Pyre sat down on a stump beside the log E.Z. was sitting on, but then wasn't sure what to say. An image of Rayne filled his mind and his hesitation dissipated. "Last night, I thought—Chaney told me that it might be possible for me to touch minds with Rayne. Is this true?"

A faint rainbow of color ebbed and flowed across E.Z.'s skin. "It usually only happens between bonded pairs, but it has been known to happen to others as well if the will is strong enough."

"Please," Pyre went down on his knees in front of the Ilezie. "Can you help me make contact with Rayne? I need to know if she's all right."

"And what if she is not all right?"

Pyre looked at him earnestly. "Then I need to know that as well. It is the not knowing that I find impossible to bear."

"Very well," E.Z. agreed. "Close your eyes. Form your thoughts like an arrow and focus on her. When you are ready, let loose your thoughts and send them flying to her. Your target is her mind."

Sitting back on his heels, Pyre let thoughts of Rayne fill his mind. When he thought the moment was right, he sent those thoughts arrowing towards where she was being kept prisoner.

"What does your mind tell you?"

"I-I-I can feel her. She's sleeping, exhausted. She is unharmed but she is very unhappy."

"Then maybe you should send her a message of hope along your link."

It was a heady feeling, being able to do this. Pyre wished she was awake and knew he could wake her with his thoughts, but she was so exhausted he did not have the heart to do so. Instead, he let his message fill her mind.

I am coming, he said. *I will find you and we will never be parted again.*

Chapter Twenty-One

From Wynne's Journal:

I do not know who came up with the name 'twice-gifted' for the children with the accelerated growth rate, but a more fitting name would be the 'twice-cursed'. Take Iara, for instance. She was of the water and her body was too immature to contain her element. She drowned in her own fluids. We have lost three more of the children to the accelerated growth in this manner — one of the water, and two of the earth. There are seven more twice-gifted remaining, but so far they seem stable. Three are of air, two are of water, one of the earth, and one, Angana, whose gift is yet to be determined. She is unlike the other twice-gifted in that her mind appears to keep pace with the development of her body. I have an uneasy feeling about her, though I cannot say why. For the most part these children are good natured, of gentle disposition and quite docile. As expected, their motor skills are slow to develop, leaving them awkward and accident prone. But though their bodies mature rapidly, their minds do not keep pace. I can only be thankful that what gifts they possess seem to be insignificant.

They stood concealed along the top of the ridge, looking down at the compound below, nestled against the cliff. The cliff was at the base of a mountain, just tall enough that its peak was surrounded by a white mist.

"It doesn't look like much," Pyre said. "Are you sure the priests have the right place?"

The single-story building was large, but crudely built, as though put up in a hurry. Made of some kind of brick that had been plastered over, it was surrounded on three sides by a double fence, unlike any fence Pyre had ever seen, the fourth side being the cliff side. The outer fence was made of twisted wire, strung between wooden poles. Then there was a large, cleared patch of earth between it and the inner fence, which was made of tall, stout poles. A guard tower sat on each of the two outward facing corners and there was movement along the top of the inner wall, probably more guards.

"What you're seeing is just a small part of it," Chaney told him. "The priests were familiar with this area long before the compound was built and they tell me there's a network of caves that lead deep into the mountain."

"Is that how we're going to get in there? Through the caves?"

Chaney shot a look at Nakeisha who was standing a few feet away, talking to one of the priests. "I hope not."

Pyre caught the look. "Why? What's the matter?"

"Nakeisha's element is the wind – she doesn't do well inside the earth. From what she tells me it's a common problem most Elementals have, not being able to tolerate their opposite. Have you never noticed you have difficulty when it comes to water?"

Shrugging, Pyre replied, "Not really, but then there's very little water for me to be exposed to, save for the hot spring in my cave. And I rather enjoyed soaking in that."

"All right everyone, gather round," E.Z. called. He waited until everyone was in place before speaking. "I have received my intelligence report and this is going to be more difficult than we'd anticipated."

"An intelligence report?" Pyre asked.

"That's correct. We have been able plant one of our own people inside the compound—"

"One of *our* people?"

"That's right. Now she—"

"A woman? You sent a woman into that place?"

"Stop interrupting!" E.Z. shot Pyre a glare.

It appeared the Ilezie was not as unflappable as he appeared. The thought was somewhat comforting. Pyre lapsed into silence, his impatience barely under control.

"As I was saying, we were able to place one of our people on the inside. From what she's been able to discover, the compound goes quite a way into the mountain. The priests tell me that approaching from the caves is impossible. They've never explored the caves fully and do not know just how far back they go."

Chaney frowned. "I would think it would be dangerous to go too far back. I've been studying the mountain the cliff is a part of. That mist at the summit? I don't think that's cloud cover, I think it's smoke. I think we're dealing with a volcano here. Tunnel in too far and you're just asking for trouble."

"What kind of trouble?" The question slipped out before Pyre could prevent it.

"The danger in tunneling in a volcanic area is you might accidentally tap into a fissure that vents gas or lava, which in turn could trigger an eruption."

"What kind of a madman would do such a thing?" Nakeisha asked, appalled.

"The same kind who would create a breeding program and kidnap innocent children," E.Z. told her.

"So how are we going to get into the compound?" Pyre asked.

"I have a plan," E.Z. said. "And the key to that plan is you, my young friend."

* * * * *

Inside the compound, a stealthy figure kept to the shadows as it moved towards the quarters where the newcomers were being kept temporarily.

"And what do you think you're doing, young man. Skulking about like a thief?"

Ravi jumped, and quickly turned, an excuse already forming in his mind. "I—oh! It's just you. You scared me half to death."

The woman in the guard's uniform grinned at him. "You really shouldn't be wandering around on your own. If it was anyone but me you'd be in serious trouble."

"But you'd never turn me in, would you, Taja?" Ravi stepped closer to her, infringing on her personal space.

"What are you doing here? Were you going to visit Rayne again?"

"You didn't answer my question. Why don't you just admit you're as attracted to me as I am to you?" He reached up cup her cheek with his palm; there was the barest hint of return pressure before she pulled away.

"Stop that! You're being ridiculous."

He raised an eyebrow. "Am I?"

"Kairavini . . ." she sighed and shook her head. "How was Rayne when you saw her?"

"Angry, afraid, I don't think I helped matters."

"Why not?"

"I told her about the breeding program and what would be expected of her. She didn't take it well."

"Imagine that," the guardswoman muttered.

"I did as you asked," Ravi said. "I made contact with the oldest of the newcomers. Now, could you answer a question for me?"

"If I can," she said warily.

"Why are you really here?" He couldn't be sure in the dim light of the corridor, but he thought she paled a shade or two.

"I—I—I don't know what you mean." She backed away a step to put some distance between them. "I'm here as a guard. Dr. Arjun needed some replacements and I needed the work."

"You're not the usual sort of guard," Ravi told her.

"What makes you say that?" She was definitely showing signs of nervousness.

"You're too compassionate, for one," he told her, taking a step towards her again. "I've seen the look on your face when you've pulled guard duty on a breeding. You call me by my name, not my number. And no other guard would allow me to get this close to them." He'd backed her up to the wall. "So tell me, what are you really doing here?"

"Tell me something first," she said, her breathing slightly erratic. "If you had a choice, would you still participate in the breeding program?"

He looked at her, puzzled. "What else would I do?"

"Your life is being stolen from you and you don't even realize it." Compassion filled her eyes. "You could do whatever you liked. You could make friends and go places; you could leave this place and never look back."

"Could I be with whomever I choose instead of having her chosen for me?"

"Yes."

"I think I would like that," he whispered, leaning closer. His lips brushed hers, eliciting a slight gasp from her. He pressed his advantage, tongue delving inside her mouth to meet and duel with hers. For just a moment she kissed him back, but then her hands were on his shoulders and she was pushing him away.

"We can't do this."

"I know," he said, breathing ragged. "But I can dream."

"Oh, Kairavini." There were tears in her eyes. "You asked why I'm really here and I'm going to tell you. Just remember if you tell anyone, I won't live long enough to regret it."

"I would never betray you Taja."

"I know." She rested a palm on his cheek. "That's why I'm telling you. That, and I think I'm going to need some help."

"Help with what?"

"I'm part of a group that intends to get the Elementals from the village out of here, and anyone else who wants to come with us."

Chapter Twenty-Two

From Wynne's Journal:
Although things have been progressing smoothly of late, I am filled with foreboding. My dreams are filled with darkness and I sense trouble coming. It is frustrating, not knowing what form it will take. It may be something as simple as a pest in the crops or as serious as one of the children losing control of their gift. Only time will make things clear and I can only hope that I will figure it out before it's too late. I curse myself for failing to contact the Ilezie in the beginning as I'd always planned. Three of the children are manifesting their gifts and are not even close to their tespiro. Perhaps this is the foreboding I have been feeling. Although this is not unheard of, nor is it always an indication that the tespiro will be a difficult one, it is disturbing nonetheless. Now, of course, it is too late to ask for aid. Even if I could be sure of the reaction of the Ilezie to the twice-gifted, I could not leave the children long enough to journey to the city. Should anything go wrong with any of the children, the villagers are ill equipped to handle it.

The rescue party set up camp in a well-screened grove almost a mile from the compound. They didn't want to risk a fire giving them away so it was cold rations for their meals. Pyre sat with his back to a tall, leafy tree. He called forth a small fire ball and let it dance from fingertip to fingertip on one hand, jump to his other hand to do the same, and then back again. It was either this or pace, and he'd already paced miles.

He was ready to snap. After hearing from his spy inside the compound, E.Z. decided to send for reinforcements. It would be another twelve hours at least until they arrived. In the meantime, who knew what was happening to Rayne and the children. He tried several times to contact her mentally, but he wasn't able to bridge the gap well enough for true communication. He was, however, able to sense her feelings, what Nakeisha said was an empathic bond, and he almost smiled at the anger he was sensing.

"That's my girl," he whispered. "Don't let them wear you down. Keep fighting."

"All right, everyone," Chaney called. "Gather round."

Pyre shook his hand and the flame disappeared. He was still amazed at how little effort it took to control his fire. It was such a relief not to live in fear of his element getting away from him.

"Reinforcements will be here in about two hours. Unfortunately it will be dark by—"

"Two hours!" Pyre blurted out before he could stop himself. "How is this possible? It took us two days to reach this place."

"It's possible because when we received your message we were already in this sector of space, waiting to rendezvous with another ship. That ship has since arrived and is sending a shuttle – something like a cargo ship, only for people. And before you ask," Chaney said, as Pyre opened his mouth again. "It has what we call a VEIL, a device that makes it invisible, so we can sneak past the authorities that don't allow space craft here."

"You cannot mean to use a space craft to fire upon the compound. It's too dangerous!" The Mother had taught them a little about ships and space and other worlds, enough to give them a deference for technology and what it could do.

"Don't worry," Nakeisha assured him. The light touch of her hand on his arm was enough to calm him down. There was a part of him that wondered how she did that. "The shuttle is only used for pick up and delivery. It is not a machine of war."

"Our spy inside the compound tells us that the children from the village are being kept in the forward part of the building," Chaney continued. "We want to keep it that way so that when we make our move Arjun doesn't have a chance to hide them further back in the tunnels. Pyre . . ."

Pyre straightened up from his slouch.

"I know you've only been in full control of your element for a few days, but how's your aim?"

"My aim?" he asked in a puzzled voice.

"I know that being a Fire Elemental you can set just about anything on fire, but can you do it at a distance?"

"I—I—I don't know. There's never been any reason to try. I've spent most of my life trying to suppress my gift, not use it."

"There's no time like the present," Chaney told him. "See that line of rocks over there?" he pointed across the clearing. "Think you can light a series of small fires in a line across them?"

Pyre looked dubiously at the rocks. Closing his eyes, he mentally sifted through the information E.Z. had implanted in his mind, ferreting out the answer. Focusing his mind, he opened his eyes again and stared at the rocks. Several bright flames appeared on the rocks, then several more, all in a straight line.

"Excellent!" Chaney said as Pyre extinguished the flames again. "Now. Here's what we're going to do."

* * * * *

They met in one of the dead end tunnels that riddled the inner part of the compound.

"How did it go?"

Ravi sighed. "It went as I expected. I spoke only to those I could trust and they are all too afraid to help."

"Even if it means they can be free?"

"You must understand, Taja, we have lived all our lives within the compound. The outside is just as frightening as staying here is. For some it is even more frightening."

She echoed his sigh. "I had hoped . . . never mind." She shook her head. "It's like you've all been conditioned to this life. It breaks my heart."

He moved closer to her. "And me? Do I break your heart?"

She reached up and cupped the side of his face. "You could quite easily break my heart worst of all," she whispered.

Leaning closer he kissed her gently, and when she didn't pull away he deepened it. For a few glorious seconds she kissed him back before exerting her iron will and pulling back. She did not, however, pull away and he took comfort in this.

"I was just a child when the compound was moved, but I still remember that day. It was terrifying. We were loaded into transports and flown to this location. The building wasn't finished yet and we had to camp out doors. I remember a lot of screaming and crying, but I also remember touching a tree – the roughness of its bark, the stickiness of the sap, the smell of it . . ."

"Oh, Ravi."

"I think freedom is something I could get used to," he said, looking down at her.

"Freedom is not something you should have to get used to," Taja told him. "It is something you should be born to. You do understand what Arjun is doing here is wrong, don't you?"

"I'm beginning to, thanks to you."

She smiled tremulously. "Good. I just wish we had time to make the others understand as well."

"I am trying, but . . ." he shrugged helplessly. "Though the others will not join us, they have promised not to hinder us. A few may even assist in the escape of the newcomers."

"At least that's something."

"What happens now?"

"Now, we get ready." Taja was all business again. She pulled a hand-drawn map of the compound from her back pocket and unfolded it. "Here's where the newcomers are quartered. We need to get them to this point here before all hell breaks loose."

"All hell?" Ravi was nervous, but determined to help.

"Yes. My friends on the outside are arranging a distraction and then they'll be breaking through the gates. At that point the priority is to get as many of the children out as possible."

"When do we start?"

"We're just wait—" she stopped, head held to one side as though listening. "We start now."

"Now? How do you know?"

She started to lead the way out of the tunnel. "I was fitted with an E.T.T., an Esper Thought Transfer device. It allows limited thought communication. I was just told that we need to get ready."

"But the guards . . ." he almost had to jog to keep up with her.

"The guards will have better things to worry about than what we're doing, trust me."

"I do trust you," he said soberly. "I wouldn't be doing this otherwise."

Taja stopped suddenly. "I know I'm asking a lot of you," she began.

He stopped her by placing his fingers to her lips. "You're asking nothing of me I'm not willing to give. Just tell me one thing . . ."

"If I can."

"I want to know what your real name is."

A smile curved her lips. "I'll tell you once we're out of here."

"Promise?"

"I promise."

Chapter Twenty-Three

From Wynne's Journal:

It has been almost a year since my last entry. Not much has changed. The children grow and thrive, the village carries on in solitude. Our location was chosen carefully so that visitors are discouraged from seeking us out. We have little to offer. Once a year a delegation takes the crops and other goods to the city near the space port for trade and this is our only contact with the world outside the village. It is just as well that this world is still relatively young, our isolation is not questioned. It surprises me how easily I have adapted to life in the village. The compound and my life there seems so long ago. Sometimes I can't help but wonder where Dr. Arjun moved the compound to, and if there is anyone left behind who cares for the welfare of the children. Is there another who is successful in smuggling children away? Perhaps there is even another village out there somewhere, hidden away from the prying eyes of the world.

Pyre stood concealed in the trees with Nakeisha and the Ilezie, looking down on the compound.

Everything was quiet. If he hadn't been watching so carefully, he would have been unable to make out the troops from the ship snaking their way into position, concealed along the front of the compound. The priests he couldn't see at all.

He knew they were here to rescue all of the Gifted stolen from the village, but the only one he could think of was Rayne. If he concentrated, he could sense some of what she was feeling – she was agitated, angry, and fearful by turns – but he was unable to achieve the full contact he had that first time.

Patience, he counseled himself. *In a short time we shall be reunited.*

"Can we count on any help from the inside?" Nakeisha asked.

E.Z. sighed. "Our operative has enlisted the aid of one of the test subjects, but the others are too afraid. They will not hinder us, but neither will they help."

"Just one?" she asked, appalled. "But there's so many of them."

"Do none of them wish their freedom?" Pyre asked in surprise.

"This is the only life they have ever known. For them the world outside of the compound is more frightening than the world within."

"I think I understand," Pyre said slowly. "It is like raising an animal in a cage. Open the cage and, as long as the animal is provided for, it remains in the cage. It has never known freedom, so cannot miss it. The cage is safe, and everything it needs is within. Without is a vast unknown, and therefore dangerous."

"Exactly," E.Z. said.

"My fire . . ." Pyre looked distinctly uncomfortable as he asked the question that was uppermost in his mind. "You are sure it will not harm any one?"

"As long as you are able to maintain it steadily then all should be well."

The plan hinged on Pyre being able to keep the fire burning not just on the compound, but in it too in order to make sure the villagers were not moved further back into the caves. If that were to happen there'd be no finding them.

"Get ready," Nakeisha said suddenly.

Pyre refocused on the compound, mentally choosing the line where he wanted his fire to go.

"Now!"

A line of fire appeared along the top of the compound where it joined to the cliffside. With the precision of someone who'd been doing this for years, Pyre was able to direct the fire downwards while containing it in a sheet.

"Good!" E.Z. encouraged him. "Now the guard towers."

Nakeisha called up her wind and sent it arrowing towards the towers. The towers exploded outwards with tremendous force.

"You only needed to knock them down, not blow them apart," E.Z. said in a slightly chiding tone of voice.

She shrugged. "Sorry."

"Now what?" Pyre asked, keeping his fires steady.

"Look," E.Z. directed.

The troops and the priests of Nishon streamed through the gates and into the compound.

"Now all we can do is wait."

Rayne was pacing her room when the alarm sounded. The shrill, piercing, noise seemed to come from all around her. Heart pounding, she stopped in her tracks, frozen in place. The lights flickered, then dimmed. She was facing her door and saw the handle jiggle slightly – someone was trying to get in.

Her paralysis broken, she backed away from the door. This wasn't the right time for a meal, which meant that whatever the reason the person on the other side of the door had for entering her room it couldn't be a good one.

"Ravi!" she exclaimed, recognizing the person standing in the doorway. "What are you doing here? What is that noise? What's going on?" With each question her voice rose a little higher.

"You have friends who have come to rescue you," he told her. "We don't have much time, we have to hurry."

"Pyre!"

The way her face lit up, Ravi felt a quick flash of envy for whoever this Pyre was. "I don't know who it is, all I know is I need to get you to the main entrance. Now hurry!"

She willingly followed as he led the way. Most of the doors along the corridor were open, the rooms empty. The lab, when they passed through it, was empty as well. There was broken glass on the floor and various liquids spilled on the tables. Whoever had left the lab, left in a hurry. Twice, when they entered the next series of hallways, Ravi pulled her into a doorway to let armed guards pass. No one stopped them though.

"Is that smoke I smell?"

"Yes. The compound is on fire."

Rayne stopped suddenly. "But . . . what about the others? Won't they be trapped? It's our duty, as Water Elementals, to help them."

"They're not trapped," he said, grabbing her arm roughly and dragging her forward. "There are tunnels that go far back into the mountain. Almost everyone is already living inside the mountain, it's just you and the rest of the villagers who were being kept in the original compound."

"The others!" Rayne was genuinely appalled that she'd forgotten about them. "We have to go back."

"They're being taken care of," he assured her. "They're probably already at the entrance."

A new explosion sounded from behind them.

* * * * *

The alarm from the compound was so loud that Pyre could hear it from the top of the ridge. He couldn't imagine what it sounded like inside. He hated waiting. Pacing back and forth along the top of the ridge he couldn't help but think of all the things that could go wrong.

"What if Arjun already moved the children into the tunnels? We'll never find them."

"Relax," Nakeisha said in her soothing voice. "E.Z.'s spy told him they already had the children headed towards the front entrance and are just going back for Rayne."

Pyre started to nod, then, "Rayne!" He could feel a sharp spike of fear from her. For a crucial second he lost control of his element. There was an explosion from the compound.

"What happened?" Nakeisha asked, staring with alarm at the compound.

"I—I—I felt her fear. I'm sorry, my fire . . ."

"Too late to do anything about it now," E.Z. said. "But I don't think it matters. Look." One long, slender finger pointed towards the compound. A stream of figures was seen leaving the building, accompanied by a few of the troops.

"I don't see—" Pyre's words were cut off as there was a rumble from the direction of the mountain. The ground trembled lightly beneath their feet.

"What's happening?" Nakeisha asked with a gasp.

"I think that dormant volcano is no longer dormant," E.Z. told her.

They looked upwards and saw the smoke coming from the mountain flowing thicker, darker, and faster.

"Did I cause this?" Pyre asked, a sick look on his face.

"No, it's just coincidence, isn't it E.Z.?"

"This is not good," E.Z. muttered. "This is not good at all!"

Chapter Twenty-Four

From Wynne's Journal:

How many years has it been since I made the trek to this place, leaving my old life behind? The children are beginning the their time of tespiro. Two of the twice-gifted, Dimytro, of the earth, and Angana, who has a mutated gift that seems to enhance others, passed through tespiro effortlessly. The third child, Pavan, of the wind, caused much damage before he could be brought under control. I have a store of the drugs we used in the lab for easing the transition, I just pray I have enough for what is to come. It seems like just yesterday that I was smuggling infants from the compound and now more than a third of them have undergone their tespiro. Given the primitive conditions I am working under it is a wonder I have not lost more, but even the death of one brings great sorrow, especially given the circumstances. Pyrphoros began his transition and, as is the case with most of the fire persuasion it boded to be a difficult one. I had prepared a cave, just outside the village, for such an occurrence and I was there with him when a second Fire Elemental, Edan, began his. I had not told anyone about the cave

*so no one knew where to find me. By the time I returned to the
village with Pyrphoros, Edan was gone.*

Rayne and Ravi were thrown to the floor by the
new explosion. As the debris began to settle, Ravi
helped her to her feet.

"Are you all right?" he asked, shouting to make
himself heard over the noise.

"I think so," she shouted back. "How about
you?"

"I'm fine. Look, just follow this passage until you
reach an intersection. Stay to the right and it'll take
you right to the entrance."

"Wait!" She grabbed his arm as he turned to go
back the way they'd come from. "What are you doing? Aren't you coming with me?"

"I can't, there's something I have to do first.
Look, I don't have time to explain. Just get to the
main entrance. There'll be a guard there, her name is
Taja. She's one of the ones sent to rescue you and the
others. Tell her . . . tell her I'm sorry."

He jerked himself free of her hold and raced back
down the corridor. Rayne stared at his retreating figure for a moment, biting her lip in indecision. A rum-
bling sound filled the air and the ground under her
feet shook slightly. The dust and smoke began to
thicken. Self-preservation won out and she fled forward towards freedom.

The intersection of the corridors wasn't too far beyond where they'd stopped and she took the right branch, as instructed. She'd only gone a few yards when she could smell fresh air. The tantalizing scent led her to an open space, a foyer of sorts, with an open door beyond. Someone was pacing to and fro in front of the door, stopping when Rayne emerged from the hallway.

"Are you Taja?" Rayne asked tentatively, poised to run.

"You must be Rayne," the woman said with obvious relief. "The others are already out there. We need to hurry before—" she broke off suddenly. "Wait a minute. Where's Ravi?"

"He went back. He wouldn't tell me why," Rayne told her. "He said to tell you he's sorry."

"Damn him!" the other woman cursed.

The ground trembled, throwing them off balance.

"Look, just go through this door and then straight through the gates to the ridge. The others will be waiting for you there."

"What about you?" Rayne asked, although from the look on the other woman's face she already knew the answer.

"I have to go after him," Taja said. The reason was in both her voice and her eyes.

"I understand," Rayne told her. "Good luck," she called, as Taja turned and raced back down the corridor.

* * * * *

Up on the ridge the rescued children were put in charge of a well-trained medical staff and taken to the transport ship. The ground shook intermittently and dust and smoke filled the air.

Pyre started at a touch on his arm. It was the Ilez-ie.

"I believe you may safely extinguish your fire," E.Z. told him.

As he did so, there came the sound of another explosion from the compound. Pyre's face paled. "Did I—"

"That one was not ours," Chaney said, joining them.

The dust and smoke in the air made it seem like twilight. The ground trembled again and flakes, like snow, drifted gently down.

"Ash," Nakeisha said, catching some on her hand.

"We need to go, now," Chaney told them.

"Not without Rayne!" Pyre said stubbornly.

"It's been too long. I'm sorry but the chances—"

"Look!" Nakeisha pointed. "There's someone down there!"

Pyre was already in motion, half stumbling, half running down the ridge to meet her. The others watched silently as the two met and embraced. Their kiss, which boded well to be of epic duration, was broken off as the ground trembled again. They needed to move.

* * * * *

Pyre could not help the misting of his eyes as he held Rayne in his arms once more. She was laughing and crying, all at the same time.

"I feared I would never see you again," she said.

"I would have moved this mountain itself to find you," he told her, kissing her again. "Come, it's not safe here."

Pyre and Rayne climbed to the top of the ridge where the others were waiting and he made the introductions. Rayne couldn't help staring at E.Z., who bore her scrutiny with good humor.

"I can't believe the Mother's message actually brought the Ilezie here. They rescued the others?"

"The rescue was a joint effort, but yes, the Gifted are safe."

"Not all them were saved," Rayne said sadly. "The twice-gifted are no more. That madman had them killed."

"Twice-gifted?" E.Z. asked.

"A few of the children had what the Mother called accelerated growth rates," Pyre explained. "We called them the twice-gifted. They were sweet-natured, for the most part, but their minds were not quite developed fully."

"More of Arjun's so-called experiments," Nakeisha said harshly. "It's bad enough he tampered with the gifts, but to tamper with the actual DNA of an unborn child . . ."

There was a series of small explosions from the compound.

"Those weren't natural," Chaney said. He was looking through a distance viewer. "And it looks like they were right along the base of the cliff. What the hell are they doing?"

"They'll be trapped in the tunnels and killed," Nakeisha said.

"Maybe Arjun would rather be killed than to be sent back to Ardraci to face trial," Chaney suggested. "And he's taking all the evidence of his insanity with him."

"No," E.Z. stated. "Uri Arjun would not give up so easily. There must be an escape route through the mountain."

"Did you see any tunnels?" Pyre asked Rayne.

She shook her head. "I only saw the room I was held prisoner in and the lab where they ran tests on me. But Ravi said many of them were living in tunnels."

"Who's Ravi?" Pyre demanded, jealousy stabbing at him.

Rayne almost smiled at the expression on his face. "He was my friend, nothing more."

"There was a guard," E.Z. said suddenly. "She was working undercover. Do you know what happened to her?"

"Taja?" Rayne asked. "She went back to find Ravi. He'd been guiding me to the entrance when he suddenly had to go back for something. I believe they were both caught in one of the explosions."

"Shouldn't we be leaving this place?" Pyre asked. Now that he had Rayne beside him, he couldn't care less about the compound. They needed to get away from the mountain before it exploded. "Where's the shuttle?"

"Between the priests, the troops and the children, the shuttle was full. It will have to come back for us," Nakeisha told him.

"If it can," Chaney muttered under his breath.

"What do you mean, if it can?" Pyre felt his fire stirring and tamped it down immediately.

Rayne looked up at him in surprise. "How did you do that?"

He smiled down at her and hugged her to his side. "You would not believe the things I am now able to do with my fire. I have complete control."

Her eyes widened. "I look forward to hearing how *that* happened."

The ground beneath them shook hard, subsiding to a series of smaller shakings after a few seconds.

"Our young friend is right," E.Z. said. "This ridge is not safe. We need to move."

There was another trembling, this time strong enough to throw them to the ground. When it was over, there were several streams of bright lava flowing down the mountain towards them. They stared, mesmerized until Chaney's voice broke their trance.

"Where'd the landing place go?" he asked.

Chapter Twenty-Five

From Wynne's Journal:

Sometimes it is so frustrating to know that answers are out there but I dare not seek them out. The second child I saved, who is called Rayne, seems to have more than one gift. At first I thought she was of the water, as her mother Namir was, but there was something underlying her gift. While the other children don't exactly shun her, they do seem wary around her, as though they sense something different about her as well. I know it is wrong of me, but I actually enjoy the mystery that Rayne presents. Further investigation shows that she is somehow able to siphon off the gifts of others. I do not know how this is possible and I wonder what my teachers would have done in this case. I wish I dared test her to see how strong this aspect of her gift is, but I feel it is more important to help her control it. I fear that should it be left uncontrolled she may unintentionally drain someone completely. I have to wonder, had she been born on Ardraci would the Ilezie have let her live?

The small group on the ridge faced the field the shuttle had used for landing. There was an ugly gash across the flat surface, and between the ridge and what was left of the field was a newly formed, deep crevasse.

"We're in serious trouble, aren't we?" Nakeisha asked.

"We've been in trouble before," Chaney said, putting his arm around her shoulders. "We'll figure something out."

One of the priests that had been left behind hurried over to E.Z. Bowing low, he spoke rapidly in a language none of them could understand.

"What's he saying?" Chaney asked impatiently.

"He says there's another place to the west that the shuttle could use for landing. The problem is, the ground is much lower. The lava will most likely reach us there before the shuttle can return."

Rayne moved off from the others and stood watching the lava inching its way towards them. Pyre followed, putting his arm around her waist as they stood together.

"It's mesmerizing, isn't it?" he said.

"When you reach out to it, what do you sense?" she asked.

"Reach out to it? Why would I—"

"Please," she said. "Try and reach out to it and tell me what you feel."

To humor her, he did as she asked. A shiver went through him. His arms dropped from around her and he took a step forward. She could see the heat waves coming off him and his eyes held flames within them.

"What do you feel?" she whispered.

"I feel . . . heat, and energy. So much energy . . . and fire. Fire such as I never dreamed possible. Fire hot enough to melt the very rock around us."

"That's enough for now," she told him. When the flames in his eyes only grew stronger, she reached out to place a hand on his arm. "Pyre, I—oh!"

She snatched her hand back in shock. It was blistered where she touched him with it. Pyre immediately shook off the pull of the lava.

"Rayne!" Gently her cradled her hand in his, horrified at the pain he'd caused. "I am so sorry. You know that I would never intentionally—"

"Hush," she told him. "It's nothing. But I have an idea. Do you remember how we worked together at the temple?"

"Yes, but it was more like you worked and I just provided a source of energy for you."

"Could we not do something similar here? Using your fire to fuel my rain to cause a storm to cool the lava?"

He pulled her to him for a kiss. "You're brilliant!" he said, releasing her again. "I think it will work, and no one need know about your true gift."

Dragging her with him, they rejoined the others.

"We're going to see if we can get higher on the ridge," Chaney told them. "There might be a landing place at a higher altitude."

"What do you think the chances are of that?" Pyre asked.

Chaney hesitated, then admitted, "Not good, really. But we might be able to spot something that we could get to."

"There's no need," Pyre told him. "Rayne and I may be able to halt the lava, at least long enough for the shuttle to return."

"Is this true?" E.Z. asked. He glided over to them and stood in front of Rayne. "I do not recognize your gift, child."

"I—I—it's water," she stammered.

His eyes narrowed slightly. "It appears more than that, but we'll let it go for now. You said you and Pyre can stop the lava?"

"Y—y—yes sir. We can use our gifts in tandem. Pyre can draw off some of the lava's heat and I can send the rain to cool it down further."

"It might not be enough to stop it entirely," Pyre said, "But it could buy us enough time for the shuttle to pick us up."

"That might just work," Nakeisha said. "If Rayne can create a storm, I can keep it in place with my wind."

The three of them looked at E.Z., who was looking faintly surprised.

"I would not have thought it possible either," Nakeisha told him, "had Wynne, the Mother, not told them that Arjun had Water and Air work together to create snow."

"Wind and Water compliment each other," E.Z. said. "It's not unheard of for complimentary elements to work together. But to add Fire . . ."

"Had I known then what I know now," Pyre said, "Things might have turned out differently at the temple."

E.Z. gave a snort. "Had you full control of your element then, I dare say none of the raiders would have lived."

He paced away to look up at the slowly approaching lave, then turned back to them. "This is unprecedented, to have three Elementals working together," he told them. "But it just might be our only chance."

* * * * *

The small group stood just above the flat clearing they were hoping to use for the shuttle to land on. On the far side of the clearing, a river of lava approached their position. Two more fiery streams were angling their way downwards, just yards away from joining the main one.

Chaney spoke rapidly into the communicator attached to his wrist, trying to get an ETA on when the shuttle would return for them. Communications were patchy, but he was able to make out enough to make sense of.

"The VEIL was damaged and the authorities are giving them trouble about returning. The High Priests of Nishon are throwing their weight around and it should only be a few minutes before they're allowed to lift off."

"Let us waste no more time then," E.Z. said. He was like a conductor of a symphony of precious instruments. "Pyrphoros, yours will be the most dangerous task. Instead of letting the fire flow from you, you will be drawing it in, as you did to quell the fires you created at the compound."

"Inhale instead of exhale," Pyre said.

"Exactly. But it will be like inhaling a river of pure energy. You must be careful not to be seduced by the heat of the lava. If you draw too much you could burn yourself up."

"How much heat will he be able to hold?" Chaney asked. To his mind, Pyre was the weakest part of the plan. If he wasn't able to draw off enough energy, then the wind and rain weren't going to do much good.

"We have no time for tests, therefore we have no way of knowing," E.Z. said. "Rayne, when Pyre begins drawing off the thermal energy of the lava you will see it begin to slow. Despite the fact that you are untrained, you seem to be able to unconsciously tap into the natural elements of this world. That must be how you were able to create such a massive storm when you and Pyrphorus were attacked at the temple."

Pyre and Rayne looked at each other. That wasn't quite the way it had been, but Rayne was not yet ready to confess to her true gift. She spent too many years hiding what she could do. The Mother's training in secrecy ran deep.

"Nakeisha, you will use your wind to keep Rayne's storm over the lava. If you could summon a cold wind that would be so much the better."

"I've never tried controlling the temperature of my wind," she said with a frown. "Is such a thing possible?" It must be possible, she realized. That would have been how Arjun was able to use Elementals to create snow.

"We'll know soon enough," E.Z. said. "Now, the three of you take your places."

Pyre stepped forward, Nakeisha on one side of him, Rayne on the other, facing the oncoming lava. With his mind he sought out the thermal energy and began drawing the heat into himself, just like he did to quench the fire he set on the compound. The Ilezie was right, it was like tapping into a river of pure fire.

The energy flowed into him faster and faster, it started to build until he wasn't sure if he could hold any more. Then he felt Rayne slip her hand into his and the pressure began to ease as she siphoned off the fire and changed it into water. The storm seemed to come out of no where, rain pelting the lava streams. Great clouds of steam hissed and billowed upwards.

So subtle was the wind at first, he didn't feel it. But the steam was moving back away from them and the clouds that were created for the rain storm remained in place. It was working! The thermal energy he was drawing on became less and less intense.

When the wind dissipated the last of the steam, the thermal energy had become a trickle and Pyre let it go. Rayne released her storm and sagged against him. Nakeisha nudged the clouds away from them and they looked up to see how they did.

The three streams had a hardened black shell over them, creating a dam that directed the lava flow to either side. They were safe . . . for now.

"Well done!" E.Z. exclaimed. The remaining priests of Nishon pointed up the mountain, talking excitedly in their own language.

Nakeisha turned and caught sight of Chaney's face as he spoke into his communicator. "What is it?"

He looked at her soberly. "The seismic readings from the mountain indicate it's close to blowing, and when it does . . . it's not just going to take out us, it's going to take out the spaceport and the city. There's a panic in the city – they're not sure the shuttle is going to make it back here."

His news sobered up the group immediately.

"Maybe we should move back up on the ridge," Nakeisha suggested after a few minutes.

She and Chaney led the way, followed by the priests, then Rayne.

Pyre still stood in the clearing, staring up at the volcano, E.Z. beside him.

I know what you are thinking, and it is too dangerous.

Pyre looked up at E.Z. *But would it work?*

E.Z. hesitated. *It is possible, but it is not likely you would survive.*

Chapter Twenty-Six

From Wynne's Journal:
It has been another pleasant interval for the village. The crops are doing well and it looks to be a plentiful harvest this year. This is a good thing as the last few harvests have not lived up to expectations. The remaining twice-gifted have all passed their tespiro easily. I cannot express what a relief this is to me. I worried for them more than the others altogether. It is my hope that now that they have passed this stage in their development their rate of growth will start to ease. Should they keep on at the rate from their infancy, they will surpass me in age before the others reach adulthood. Over half of the children have passed through tespiro now. There have been no major problems, but something odd is going on with several of the boys. It's nothing I can put my finger on, but they seem nervous, almost frightened. But of what I cannot say. And then there is Angana. There is a slyness to the girl that bears watching. Perhaps it is nothing, but I have a bad feeling about her, as though she is up to something.

"Where's Pyre?" Rayne asked as E.Z. joined the small group on the ridge.

"He . . ." the Ilezie hesitated. "He wishes to try and subdue the volcano."

"He can do that?" Chaney asked in surprise.

"He is a Fire Elemental, one of the most powerful I have ever encountered. However . . ." he shrugged. "I do not know."

Rayne looked past them, down to where Pyre stood alone, ash falling on him like snow. "No, it's too dangerous," she said. "You can't let him!"

"He is a grown man, and a powerful Elemental. It is not my place to tell him what he can and can not do."

"Well I can!" She started to push past them but Nakeisha put a restraining hand on her arm.

"You care for him, just as he cares for you. Would you deny him this chance to save not only your life but the thousands of lives in the city and space port?"

Rayne looked at her, tears in her eyes. "But what if he dies trying?"

"Then we shall all perish," Nakeisha said bluntly.

* * * * *

At the bottom of the ridge, Pyre closed his eyes and reached out with his senses. He could feel the heat from the lava streams and followed them with his mind, upwards to where they emerged from the mountain and then back down into the heart of the volcano. Draining these small streams would have little effect on the imminent eruption, he needed to go deeper.

Down into the earth his mind travelled until it reached the magma chamber far beneath his feet. This was it, the heart of the volcano. He let the essence of the molten rock fill him, and then using only his mind he began to pull.

The thermal energy resisted at first, then started to flow into him. It was like standing in the heart of a flame. Joy filled him at the sheer power of his element. Faster and faster the fire filled him. Dimly he heard Rayne calling his name but he was beyond caring. He was one with his element now. Nothing mattered but the Fire.

The flow of energy from the volcano was slowing. This was unacceptable! He needed more energy.

He sent his mind questing further downwards, following the hidden trail of the thermal energy even further below. It was elusive, almost out of reach. But he was Pyre, god-like in his control of the Elemental Fire. He touched the molten core of the planet.

* * * * *

Chaney kept his eyes glued to the instrument in his hand. "Whatever he's doing, it's working. The thermal energy from inside the volcano is dropping."

E.Z. moved closer to the edge of the ridge.

"What is it?" Nakeisha asked.

"I sense . . . something is not right."

"That's it! He's done it!" Chaney said triumphantly. "The volcano is quieting, dormant again. I've never seen anything like it – it's absolutely incredible!"

"And yet his energy is still building," E.Z. said.

They watched in horror as flames engulfed Pyre. He'd become a living, breathing torch.

"Pyre!" Rayne screamed.

Nakeisha held her back. "No, it's too dangerous."

"You don't understand! I have to go to him!"

"E.Z., what's happening?" Chaney asked.

"I have never witnessed such a thing," the Ilezie whispered. "I would not have thought it possible."

"What's not possible?"

"He has touched the planet's thermal core and is drawing energy directly from it. If he is not stopped, he will tear the planet apart."

Chaney pulled out his laser pistol and aimed it down the slope.

"No," E.Z. said quickly. "That is not the answer. If you shoot him there is no telling what will happen. The energy may just explode out of him and destroy the planet anyway."

"Then how do we stop him?"

Rayne struggled in Nakeisha's grasp. "I must go to him, he'll listen to me."

"Look at him, it's too dangerous!"

"You don't understand, I can help him!" She broke free of Nakeisha's hold.

"Rayne, no!"

Before anyone could stop her, she was racing down the slope to Pyre. She stopped a few feet away. It was a true, Elemental Fire surrounding him – pale, translucent flames of palest yellow and orange, streaked with blue and red.

"Pyre," she whispered, unable to look away from his terrible beauty. "You will undo all the good you have done if you do not stop absorbing the thermal energy."

He looked at her, flames filling his eyes, and it was as though a stranger looked at her. "I am Pyrphoros, god of fire. I take what I wish."

"No," she said, taking a step closer. "You are Pyre and you must stop this madness."

Something flickered in his eyes. "The power . . . it is mine to do with as I please." The ground trembled beneath their feet.

"You take what is not yours," she told him, taking another step closer. "It makes you no better than a thief. You steal the very life from this world."

"No, I—"

There was uncertainty in his flame-filled eyes now and she pressed her advantage. Moving close enough to him that she could almost touch him, she looked up at him, unafraid.

"You must replace what you have stolen, else we will die before we have had the chance to grow old together."

"Rayne?" Flames still filled his eyes, but sanity had returned.

"Yes, my love."

His voice died to a whisper. "Oh, the power, Rayne. Such power as I had never imagined before."

"Please, Pyre, you must release the energy back into the planet's core."

"Yes, I . . . I don't know if I can."

"I have faith in you," she said, and took the final step towards him, stepping into the fire.

She put her arms around him and his fire did not burn her. Instead, it embraced her as well. She could feel it dancing along her skin; she breathed it into her lungs. All that mattered was that they were together again, and live or die, nothing would separate them ever again.

"It's too much, I can't hold it all," he said.

"Then release it, as you learned to do with your fire."

"I—I can't. There's so much power that if I release it all at once I will make matters worse."

"Then let me help you," she said.

She reached with her mind and tapped into his power, as she had so many times in the past. Her mouth opened in a soundless scream. It was like plunging her hands into a river of molten lava. Without hesitation she began to channel the energy into a storm.

For Pyre it was like having a pressure valve released. As the weight of all that power began to ease, he was able to start transferring thermal energy back into the core of the planet. The tremors ceased and he cut off the flow, not wanting to overload the core.

Still he was filled with energy.

The storm raged around them; lightning striking, rain pelting down. Rayne reluctantly stopped pulling energy from Pyre. The storm was already far greater than any she had ever seen before. Much more and they would be swept away by it.

"The planet's core is stable again," E.Z.'s voice cut easily through the chaos around them. Pyre and Rayne were startled apart. They hadn't realized the others had joined them.

"But the rest of the energy," Pyre said. He could feel it roiling inside him, almost overwhelming in intensity. "What do I do with it?"

"I suggest you release it."

Chapter Twenty-Seven

From Wynne's Journal:

I blame myself, as much as anyone, for what has transpired. I knew there was something amiss with Angana but I did not keep as close an eye on her as I should have. Her gift was something that could have been of great benefit. But instead she perverted her power, preying on the weak, newly turned boys, causing them to think their gifts had gone out of control, something each one of the gifted fears. Who knows how many boys she might have ruined she had not tried her tricks on Pyrphoros. His gift of fire needed no enhancing from anyone and the resulting conflagration consumed them both. Pyrphoros was never an outgoing child and now he has withdrawn from even his foster mother. He blames himself for Angana's death and nothing anyone says will convince him otherwise. He talks about leaving the village and living by himself up on the mountain. I cannot imagine what the isolation of living alone on the mountain would be like. He was the first of the children I rescued, and so is close to my heart, but his importance is so much

*more than that. I have seen the future, and he has a vital part
to play.*

The elemental fire surrounding Pyre flared
brighter with his efforts at containing the excess
thermal energy within him. Rayne dared not siphon
off any more of his gift, the storm raging around
them was already devastating in intensity. It was going
to cause enormous damage if it reached the city and
spaceport.

Already the area around them was ravaged. Lightning struck, tearing great gouges into the earth, split-
ting trees and setting them on fire. Fires were lit, only
to be doused again by the rain.

Nakeisha raised a wind to try and redirect the
storm, but it was having no effect. She concentrated
hard, trying to tap into the primal energy of the storm
but it eluded her. "I don't understand it," she said.

E.Z. glanced upwards at the maelstrom of lightning and rain. It was like they were standing in the eye
of a hurricane. The area where they stood was relatively calm, while all around them was chaos.

"There is something wrong with this storm. The
energy is wrong."

"It is my fault," Rayne said suddenly. "The energy was too great." She was white faced and shiver-
ing from the after effects of sharing, for even a few
seconds, the enormous power Pyre was holding at
bay.

"Not . . . your . . . fault," Pyre gasped. The energy was almost like a separate entity, one that did not like being held at bay. It struggled to escape and he struggled to keep it contained.

"This has something to do with your other ability, doesn't it?" E.Z. asked.

"Yes, I . . ." Rayne glanced at Pyre, then resolutely faced the Ilezie. "I have a deviant ability. I am able to take the gifts of others and . . . change them."

"Change them how?" Nakeisha asked.

"I . . . do not have good control of my element, but I can take from another's gift and turn it into my own."

"You mean you can siphon off other elements and turn them into some kind of water?"

"Yes," Rayne said miserably. Would she survive this, only to once again be facing fear and contempt? Maybe she and Pyre could go back to his cave to live out their days in peace. Or maybe the Ilezie would just destroy her.

"I've never heard of such a gift," Nakeisha said in astonishment. "This is truly amazing."

"Unfortunately, I have no say in what form the gift will take once I have released it again. Usually it falls as rain, the stronger the energy, the more intense the rainfall."

"And you helped Pyrphoros by drawing off some of his energy and created the storm?" Chaney asked.

"Yes, but it was so intense, it happened so fast . . ."

". . . that the storm holds more of his element than yours," E.Z. finished for her. "And with the amount of energy Pyrphoros still contains within him, he is acting as an anchor for it."

"Can't you just take more of his energy?" Chaney asked Rayne.

She shook her head. "Look around you. I dare not, else there would be no stopping this storm."

"What do we do?" Chaney asked.

"We can do nothing," E.Z. said. "It is up to Pyrphoros. He will release the energy within him, or it will consume him. Either way it will release the storm."

"You cold-hearted bastard!" Rayne turned on him, fists clenched. "Don't you even care that he might die?"

"We might all die," E.Z. told her calmly.

"Stop it!" Pyre said. "I . . . can . . . do this."

Rayne turned to him, eyes bright with unshed tears. *I love you*, she projected with her mind.

He met her gaze and his resolve strengthened. *And I you*, he told her. *Now step back, in case this should go badly.*

No, she shook her head. *If you die, we die together. I will not be parted from you again.*

* * * * *

Release it, the Ilezie had said – it sounds so easy, Pyre thought. But release it how? He needed a channel of some kind. If he released it into the planet's core he chanced overloading the core and making it unstable. He could not release it back into the mountain or they'd be right back where they started. And Rayne could not take any more from him or her storm would devastate the whole planet. He could think of no way to safely release the energy.

You think too small, a voice he recognized as E.Z.'s filled his mind.

What do you mean?

Look up.

Puzzled, Pyre did as the Ilezie suggested. He looked upwards, up through the funnel the storm had created, up past where the clouds should be, up into the night sky. The stars glittered above them, unchanged by what was taking place below.

Yes! I understand now!

Pyre refocused his attention on the inferno swirling inside him. Again, it was like the energy was sentient and knew what he was planning. It fought his control. The elemental fire began giving off sparks around him, causing the others to draw back.

"I am Pyre," he said between clenched teeth. "I am the master here, not you."

He gathered up every ounce of his self will and hurled the energy up through the funnel of the storm.

Unable to hear Rayne scream his name, he stood in the heart of the blaze, fueling the fire with energy that sent it shooting straight up into space. In that moment he was not just Pyre, he was the Elemental Fire as well.

When the last of the energy from the volcano had been expelled, the fire winked out, leaving Pyre swaying on his feet. His clothes had been burned away, but the rest of him was untouched. Eyes wide in his gaunt face, he opened his mouth to speak, then collapsed.

"Now that's what I call impressive," Chaney said in the ensuing silence.

Nakeisha was ready with her wind. The second the energy tethering the storm to Pyre disappeared, she threw a protective shield around them and pushed the storm away, towards the other side of the mountain.

The moment Pyre collapsed, Rayne was on the ground cradling his head in her lap. One of the priests handed her a blanket to wrap around him.

"He lives," she said, tears running unnoticed down her face. "But I cannot awaken him."

"Let him be, child," E.Z. advised her. "He deserves a rest."

* * * * *

When Pyre awoke, he at first had no idea what had happened, let alone where he was. Slowly, bits and pieces began coming back to him. Opening his eyes, he sat up in bed and looked around. He was in an unfamiliar bedroom, much like the one he'd been given during his brief stay on the ship, only this one was much larger.

He should have been feeling tired, or at the very least weakened, but he felt . . . fine. It was a surprising feeling. Holding out his hand he summoned his fire. It came easily to him and he grinned before letting it wink out again.

There were two doors to the room, one open and one closed. The closed one probably held sanitary facilities. He listened, but couldn't hear any noise coming from inside it. With a frown, he got up and pulled on the robe lying across the end of the bed. Where was Rayne?

Stepping through the door into the main room of the suite, he looked around curiously. It was much larger than the room he'd been given previously, was it even the same ship? The room was comfortable looking, but did not hold what he was looking for. Skirting a large sofa, he breathed a sigh of relief when he spotted two packs resting on a table – his and Rayne's. But where was she?

As he picked up his pack, determined to go find someone and demand information, the door to the suite slid open and Rayne entered, carrying a tray filled with food. Her eyes lit up as she saw him standing beside the table.

"You're awake!" she said, blushing at having blurted out something so obvious. "You've been asleep for two days." She set the tray on the table beside her pack. "How are you feeling?"

"I—" The words stuck in his throat as he drank in her presence. She was so very beautiful. Gone were the shadows under her eyes, the lines of strain, the worry. But there was a faint shyness in her look, as though she was unsure of her welcome.

Without a word he pulled her into his arms and kissed her, banishing any reservations between them. Her arms crept up around his neck and she pressed closer. His back pack dropped unnoticed to the floor.

"The Gifted?" he asked, between frantic kisses.

"Safe," she gasped, kissing him back.

"Your sister?"

"She is safe as well."

"Good." He swept her up in his arms and carried her towards the bedchamber.

"You need to eat," she protested faintly, as he laid her down on the bed and started undressing her.

"Food is not what I am hungry for," he told her.

Her protest had been half-hearted at best and she couldn't help the half-smile that curved her lips as he impatiently tossed the last of her clothing aside and removed his robe.

"I confess, food is not what I hunger for either," she whispered, reaching for him.

Chapter Twenty-Eight

From Wynne's Journal:
I have been having a recurring vision of the future, unlike any I have ever had before. There is a world, a strange and alien place, and yet it feels familiar to me. There is a sense of great age and great power here; it makes me tremble but I am not afraid. There are five moons in the amber sky: silver, ocher, pale blue, pale green, and the final one a combination of all the other colors, swirling together. They have circled this world from the dawn of time, each dancing to its own tune. But soon, very soon, their dance will become synchronized, and should that happen it will mean the end of not only this world, but worlds beyond worlds. Somewhere on this world is a vast sea of thick, churning fluid. It is not water, nor any other liquid I can put a name to. Perhaps it is not liquid at all but gas. Out on this sea lies an island, and upon this island is a temple dedicated to the One. But it is not one who can save this world, it is five who become one. This vision fills me with both fear and hope, but I do not know why.

Pyre lay down beside her, leaning most of his weight on one elbow. He stroked his free hand down her neck, her breast, her torso, and then back up again. Her body shivered in response.

"I have missed you," he said.

She didn't answer, instead she threaded her hands through his hair and pulled his face down to hers for a kiss. To Pyre it was like a cool drink after a long day. She was soft and pliant, like a gently flowing stream and he drank deeply.

Rayne could feel his erection pressing hot and hard against her thigh. Releasing her grip on his hair, she slid her hands over his shoulders and down his back, one of them eventually working its way around and down to that which she most hungered for. He jerked in surprise as she grasped him.

"I want to go slowly," he protested, lifting his head. "I want to make this last."

"We can go slowly another time. This time I cannot wait for slow!"

Gone was the quiet water flowing over the riverbed, in its place was a lava stream, ferocious and powerful. Pyre groaned, her fire feeding his own. He kissed her fiercely and grabbed her wrists in his hands, pulling her arms above her head. Keeping her wrists trapped with one hand, he slid the other downwards, slipping between her restless thighs. Her hips bucked upwards as he slid his fingers through her soft, damp folds, one finger delving inside her.

His head dipped down and caught her breast, sucking the nipple deep into his mouth, laving with his tongue, nipping with his teeth. A second finger joined the first.

Her hips arched upwards again. "Pyre, please!"

He stroked slowly in and out, brushing his thumb lightly over the hard little nubbin just above. Her hips undulated in a counter-rhythm, her arms straining against his hold. When he took away his hand, she whimpered in protest. Nudging her knees further apart, he guided himself into her tight, wet sheath.

It was like coming home. He held still for a moment, wanting to savor the sensation, but she would have none of that. She arched upwards with her hips, wrapping her legs around his waist. He let go of her wrists and she slid her hands into his hair again, then down his shoulders and back.

They moved together in a steady, harmonious, rhythm. Her fingers dug into his back, trying to pull him closer to her. He kissed her again, then trailed kisses down her neck.

"Faster!" she urged.

Pyre picked up the pace – faster, harder. He was close, so close. Slipping a hand between their sweat slickened bodies, he sought out that tight bud of pleasure between her legs, caressing it lightly. She arched upwards, crying out his name, and came apart in his arms. Two more strokes and he tumbled over as well.

He hung over her, trying to let his arms braced on either side of her take most of his weight as they panted for breath. Kissing her gently, he moved beside her and pulled her into his arms so that she lay draped half over him. She nestled into his arms with a contented sigh.

"What happens now?"

Rayne sighed again, resting her head on his shoulder. "The others have been given a choice to remain Gifted or have their gifts blocked."

Pyre frowned. "I thought E.Z. said it could not be done after *tespiro*."

"Four of the others have yet to pass their *tespiro*. Of the remainder, only three, besides us, have gifts strong enough to make the procedure dangerous."

"And then what? Where do we go from here?"

She sighed and pulled away from him, sitting up in the bed. Pyre sighed as well and reached for his robe. Apparently, play time was over. Rayne found a robe as well and followed him out into the main room. She went over to stare out the view port and he came up behind her, putting his arms around her.

"What is it?" he asked, resting his chin on her shoulder.

She leaned back into his warmth. "So much has happened in so short a time. It was not that long ago that my whole world was the village and life in the village. My future was so simple."

"And now?"

"Now everything is . . . not so simple."

"I understand," he said, heart heavy. "You have many choices before you and no longer wish to be tied to one man. I—"

Turning in his arms, she smacked him on the chest. "That is not what I am saying! My feelings for you have not changed. Unless it is you . . ." her voice trailed off in uncertainty.

"My feelings have not changed either. You are the missing piece of my soul." He dipped his head down and kissed her.

"Good," she said, somewhat breathlessly when he released her. "See to it you remember that."

He grinned. "If I do, you'll just have to remind me."

She led him over to the sofa and cuddled close when he sat down beside her.

"A message was sent to the Ardraci home world," she told him. "They were most welcoming and there are families awaiting those who still need guidance."

"That's good news. Even if the fire did not spread to the rest of the village it is no longer the safe haven it once was."

"No." She shivered. "They are searching for Dr. Arjun and the rest of his people, but so far there has been no trace of them."

"Surely they perished inside the mountain?"

"The Ilezie does not believe so."

"What happens now?" He repeated his question from earlier.

"Of those who chose to have their gift blocked, three wish to continue to Ardraci where they will be welcomed, and five have chosen to return to the city, to make their way to other villages. Those who do not wish their gift blocked are going to Ardraci for training, including Tanwen."

He waited patiently, knowing there was more.

"She isn't really my sister, you know," she said, fingers smoothing down the material of her robe. "We only had the same foster parents. Dr. Arjun's records have been destroyed so we have no way of knowing who, exactly, our parents were, or if they were willing participants in his program."

"Does it really matter?"

"I suppose not, although it might have been nice to truly have a sister, or a brother out there."

"So where are we headed? To Ardraci for your training?"

She shook her head. "We have been given another option. The Ilezie, E.Z., has offered to train me himself. My gift is unique and he believes only an Ilezie can train me properly in its use."

"That makes sense, I guess," Pyre said. "What do you wish to do?"

"There is a part of me that wishes for us to return to your cave on the mountain and live out our lives in peace," she said honestly. "But there is another part of me that wonders what else is out there."

"Then it's settled," he told her, putting an arm around her shoulders and pulling her towards him. "We stay here and let E.Z. train you."

"But what about a home?"

"As long as we are together, the whole universe will be our home."

About the Author

Carol Ward always believed she was meant to be a writer of short stories, however her stories tended to be rather long. They also tended to have a romantic thread running through them. Finally caving in to the inevitable, she embraced her genre and began writing novels of fantasy/science fiction adventure with a dash of romance thrown into the mix. She has never regretted it.

Living with her husband and four cats in Cobourg, Ontario, she writes a variety of prose: non-fiction, flash fiction, short stories, and novels – in a variety of genres: humour, horror, contemporary, romance, science fiction, and fantasy. She's also a prolific poet.

You can visit Carol on her blog at:
http://www.randomwriterlythoughts.blogpot.com
     on Facebook at:
http://www.facebook.com/pages/Carol-R-Ward-Author/308347952512637
and on Twitter at:
http://www.twitter.com/CarolRWard

Other Books by the Author

An Elemental Wind

13827621R00136

Made in the USA
Charleston, SC
03 August 2012